DOCTOR'S SECRET BABY

COLE BROTHERS BOOK THREE

CRYSTAL MONROE

LET'S STAY IN TOUCH!

Join my newsletter!

You'll receive updates on new releases, freebies, and the opportunity to join my ARC (advance reader copy) team!

Sign Up Now!

https://mailchi.mp/4f480a01f207/crystal-monroe

ONE

ETHAN

"What'll it be, Ethan?" Tim, the bartender, asked. I sat down on the stool, cracking my neck and rolling my shoulders to release tension.

"The usual."

"Want to try something new? The cook's got a new jalapeño burger he's asking everyone to try. I think it's too dangerous, though. That thing burns like a bitch. Whaddya say? You man enough?"

"Sure, why not," I said.

Tim grinned and called back the order for my too-dangerous burger. He poured my beer while I rubbed my eyes.

"Rough day?" he asked.

"When isn't it?"

Tim set the beer down in front of me with a nod. I was glad he didn't pry. Between my four nosy brothers and the small town full of gossips I lived in, I got plenty of that already.

I leaned back against the barstool and closed my eyes for a moment. I'd lost a patient today. It was an occupational hazard—as doctors, we couldn't save all of them. And in the ER, we saw a lot of bad shit. But I hated it when we lost one. All life had value, and when I couldn't pull them through, it felt personal.

I needed a cold beer, a burger that would fill at least one of the empty spots inside of me, and some time to unwind.

Maybe, if I was lucky, I could find a nice girl to help ease the tension.

Everyone around The Tavern tonight was a local. I didn't do locals, not in this small town. I didn't want to have to face them again the next day and explain why I hadn't called. I didn't want to be *that* guy. All I needed was an escape, but women didn't get that. Everyone in North Haven wanted to get serious if they weren't already.

And I wasn't ready for serious.

It was easier to hook up with tourists. They already knew they were just passing through. It wasn't necessary to explain the fine print. It was a good night together, a wave goodbye when they walked away, and that was the end of it.

Simple.

I took a long sip of my beer and leaned my elbows on the bar.

"Are we doing the fifties again?" I complained when Elvis's "Hound Dog" started blaring over the speakers that hung above the bar.

"Hey, you leave Elvis alone!" someone called from the back. The comment was tailed by a burst of laughter.

I shook my head and despite my dislike, tapped my foot along to the beat.

"Oh, God, I haven't heard this song in ages!" a woman said as she walked in, hopping onto a barstool two seats down from me. "Gotta love Elvis, huh?"

"You bet," Tim said with a grin, offering me a sly glance. "What can I get you, honey?"

"Vodka tonic," she said.

"It's on me," I said.

She glanced at me, nodding, a smile spreading slowly over her features.

"That's kind of you."

I lifted a finger, tipping an imaginary hat to her.

God, she was a looker. Blonde hair that hung to just below her shoulder. Tinged with pink. *Strawberry* blonde, they called it. And she was sweet as sugar, I was willing to bet. Her eyes were bright green, and a smile played around the corners of her mouth.

"Do you have anything good to eat around here?" she asked, looking at the menu Tim had pushed in front of her.

Just as she asked, my burger and fries arrived from the kitchen.

"Oh, that looks pretty good," she murmured.

"You're going to die a slow death," Tim chuckled. "I hear it burns on the way in and on the way out."

The blonde gasped, adequately horrified.

"Don't mind him," I chipped in. "He's not used to being around beautiful women."

She rolled her eyes. "Can you be any more cliché? How many women have you used that line on?"

"None where it rang true."

She giggled. "I don't know why men think flattery will get them what they want."

I turned, amused. "And what do you think it is I want?"

"Companionship," she said. "Isn't that what they call it these days?"

I chuckled. "I believe that's exactly what they call it."

She nodded. "Well, I'm not here for companionship.

I've had just about enough of that. I'm *sans* companion right now, and I prefer to keep it that way."

Ah. Post breakup. I shifted a little closer.

"He's an asshole," I said.

Her eyes glittered, her mouth tugging into that smile that looked like it was perpetually on the verge of a promise.

"Yeah? You know him?"

"No, but I don't have to. If he let you slip through his fingers, he's an idiot." I took a sip of my beer.

She laughed, and it was like chimes skipping around me. God, I didn't want it to stop.

"You're a smooth talker."

I nodded. "Comes with the territory."

"Really? What territory?"

"I'm in the business of making people happier."

She thought about that for a minute. "It doesn't sound like an easy task."

"No, it isn't. Will you let me try it on you?"

Her eyes glittered again. "What makes you think you have what it takes?"

I grinned at her. "Oh, honey, I *know* I have more to offer than you can handle."

She laughed again, and my cock twitched in my pants. God, what was it about her? She had a zest for life that made me want to know more. So much more.

"Have you decided?" Tim asked after having filled another drink order on the other side of the bar.

"Yeah," she said, looking me in the eye. "I'll have the same."

I laughed and popped a fry into my mouth.

"Care if I sit a little closer?" I asked.

She gestured to the open barstool next to her.

I moved my plate closer before shifting over to the next

stool and took another sip of my beer. Her vodka tonic had arrived while we'd been bantering back and forth, and she sipped it through a straw.

"What do you do?" I asked.

"I'm in the business of picking up slack," she said vaguely.

I liked this game. I hadn't told her my line of work, and she didn't tell me hers. It kept things mysterious. I imagined she lived in some city a few hundred miles away. She must have been in my little town on business or maybe visiting family.

"It sounds like hard work."

She groaned. "You have no idea."

"You could always switch career paths," I said. "Something new."

She looked at me, a smile playing around her mouth, eyes dancing with laughter.

"It's always easier said than done, isn't it?" She shook her head. I wondered what her hair would feel like if I ran my fingers through it. "I love what I do, truth be told. Long hours, hard work, but it all pays off in the end."

I nodded. "Yeah, I get that, too."

She smiled at me.

I bit into my burger, chewed, swallowed.

"This isn't so bad," I said.

I bit off another chunk.

"Holy shit."

I gasped and grabbed for my beer.

"What?" she asked with a giggle.

"It's hot."

"It can't be that bad."

I shook my head. "No, you're right." More beer. God, I was going up in flames. "It's worse."

She laughed. I loved the sound, but she was enjoying herself at my expense. Dammit, this burger was too dangerous for sure.

"How are you holding up?" Tim asked with a grin.

"Fine," I gasped and practically downed most of my beer.

"I never got your name," the blonde said.

"Ethan," I said. "For when you need to pick out my tombstone."

She laughed. "Here lies Ethan, who died a slow death. By jalapeño."

I groaned, and she giggled again. Her burger arrived.

"Don't eat that," I said, hanging on the bar, struggling to hold onto the last shred of manliness I had left. "Allow me to save your life."

She offered me big eyes. "I'm sure I can take care of myself."

She bit into the burger, eyes locked on mine the whole time. And I swear, despite the meltdown I was experiencing, the way she looked at me was hot as hell.

She frowned and looked at the burger she'd just bitten into, chewing.

"It's not that bad," she said.

I blinked at her. "Wait for it."

She took another bite. Kept chewing. And another. And another.

"Are you fucking kidding me?" I asked.

She blinked at me, surprised, and swallowed.

"It's not that bad," she giggled. "It's a little spicy, sure."

"A *little* spicy?"

Tim burst out laughing.

"So, a woman has to show you how it's done, bro," he remarked. "Well, that's not something you see every day."

"Who are you?" I asked.

She giggled. "Piper."

"I think I'm going to have to buy you another drink, Piper."

"Why's that?"

"I need to save a little of my masculinity. If I pay, it will remind us both that I'm still the man in this equation."

She burst out laughing, shaking her head.

"There's nothing wrong with being *sensitive,* Ethan." Her eyes danced with pleasure at my humiliation, and I swear to God I'd never been more turned on.

I bought her another drink. And downed another beer. It didn't help. I had to finish the rest of the burger because I would look like I pussy if she could and I couldn't.

The more I drank, the more I relaxed. And Piper became more talkative, telling me something about a Buddhist meditation practice that I didn't catch. I kept staring at her mouth. Whenever she said something interesting, I wanted to kiss her. Which was all the damn time.

"What?" she asked, and I realized she'd stopped talking.

"You're beautiful," I said.

She blushed. When last had I seen a woman blush? These days, they seemed to take compliments as if it was expected.

"You can't say that, you're drunk," she said.

"So are you."

She pulled up her shoulders. "Go figure."

I leaned a little closer, eyes on her lips. She didn't pull away. I brushed my lips against hers before I kissed her, and she sighed against my lips. I slid my tongue into her mouth, and my cock was rock hard in my pants, begging for a release.

"Do you want to go somewhere a little less crowded?" I asked.

"No," she said, leaning away from me.

Dammit.

She fidgeted. "It's just... I'm not usually the type to go home with a guy I just met."

"I get it," I said, leaning back on the bar. "No worries."

She twirled her empty glass for a moment, thinking. Then she took a breath and looked up.

"Actually..." She smiled at me. "Yeah. I do. I just found this cute little place. Come home with me?"

I nodded, touching my fingertips to her cheek before paying up the last of what I owed for our drinks.

We left the Tavern together. She climbed into her car, and I followed her in mine, driving through North Haven. The place she'd gotten was modest, on the edge of town, almost in the wilderness but not quite. It was quiet but not secluded.

Quaint. I didn't know they still did vacation rentals like these.

I followed her inside. As soon as the door shut, I kissed her again, wrapping my arms around her waist and pulling her against me. I ground my hips against hers, letting her feel my erection, how much I wanted her.

She moaned.

I nuzzled her neck, drawing circles on her skin with my tongue. She ran her hands up and down my arms, gasping. I tugged her shirt lower, kissing the skin of her chest, moving down, down, down to the swell of her breasts.

She gently nudged me away, crossed her arms over her torso, and pulled her shirt over her head, dropping it to the floor.

"Easier access," she said.

I reached for my buckle and undid it, unzipping my pants. I grinned at her.

"Easier access."

She smiled at me and ran her hand down the front of my pants, brushing against my stiff cock, grazing it through the material of my boxers. My cock twitched in response.

I focused on her breasts, pulling the cups of her bra down. I sucked one nipple into my mouth, cupping the other breast, squeezing and massaging. She moaned louder and pushed her hand into my boxers, wrapping her fingers around my shaft. I groaned when she did.

"God, you're big," she whispered.

I chuckled around her nipple.

"Sorry, you probably hear that all the time," she said.

"Less than you might think."

"Maybe they're speechless," she said.

I laughed.

Everything was so smooth with her, so easy. I'd had a lot of one-night stands, and none of them had been this comfortable.

I kissed her again, and she pumped her hand up and down my cock. I wanted to fuck her so badly, it was driving me crazy.

I fiddled with her jeans.

"Just push them down. They're stretch," she said.

I nodded and did exactly that so they pooled around her ankles. She kicked the jeans away, her ballerina flats with them.

She had a smoking hot body. I stood back to admire her curves. Breasts the size of melons, wide hips, a narrow waist. She was built like a doll.

She reached for me, pulling my shirt up. If I was staring,

she could, too. I pulled up my shirt and she raised her eyebrows.

"Seriously?" she asked.

"What?"

"Where do they make guys like you? You're chiseled."

I shook my head, laughing. "You're stroking my ego."

"Yeah, you're standing too far away for me to stroke your cock."

I laughed and took a step closer again. She reached for me, cupping me in her small hand, and went to work.

I groaned. She was fucking good with her hands.

Just when I thought it couldn't get any better, she dropped to her knees and pulled down my pants, releasing my cock from the constraints of my boxers. She looked up at me, all innocence, and sucked the tip of my cock into her mouth.

I moaned and pushed my hands into her hair. It was silky, smooth, *perfect*.

She pushed my cock all the way into her mouth, swirling her tongue around the bottom of my shaft as she pulled back out. I groaned, tilting back my head, angling my hips forward. She bobbed her head faster and faster. Her hand came up and she cupped my balls while she sucked me off.

Sexual fucking *bliss*.

"You're going to make me lose my load if you keep doing that, babe," I said.

She moved her eyes up to look at me, lips still around my cock, and God, if I didn't come right then and there.

But she pulled back, and I fell out of her mouth.

"I guess you'll just have to do it inside of me, then."

My jaw nearly dropped. She was sexy as hell, sharp,

funny, and she had a dirty mouth when it came to the bedroom.

Fuck me.

I pulled her closer and kissed her. She wrapped her arms around my neck, and I pulled her tightly against me, my cock pushing up against her lace panties. Those were going to have to go. As well as that bra.

I unclasped it and pulled it off, dropping it to the floor. I stepped out of my jeans and kneeled to pull down her panties. With her pussy at face height, her scent was intoxicating. It took everything I had not to tip her over and devour her.

But I wanted to be inside her.

I found my jeans, fished for my wallet, found a condom. Safety first.

She glanced at me when I ripped the foil and rolled the condom over my cock.

I took her hand and led her to the couch. I didn't know where her main bedroom was, and she didn't protest when we collapsed in a tangle of limbs, my tongue in her mouth, cock against her stomach. I kissed her, running my hands over her naked body.

She was such a turn-on.

Her legs fell open for me, and I positioned myself between them.

"How drunk are you?" I asked.

"Drunk enough to know I want this. Badly. Not so drunk that it's an issue."

I grinned and slid into her.

She moaned when my cock filled her up. God, she was *tight*. Her body clamped down around my cock, and I paused, taking two deep breaths to fight off my pending orgasm. I was so close to the edge, and she was so hot. *Shit.*

Drinking and fucking was a bad combo for my stamina. Especially with her.

"I wasn't kidding when I said you're so big," she said in a hoarse voice.

"Bad?"

She shook her head. "No, sweetie. *Good.*"

I chuckled and slowly backed out of her. She moaned as I did. I slid out until only the tip was in before I slid back in again. Slowly, carefully. So she could get used to me. So she could want me. Crave me. *Beg* for me.

"You're teasing me," she gasped when I continued to slide in and out of her, achingly slowly.

"Yeah," I said with a grin. "What about it?"

She moaned again.

"I want more," she said.

"More what?"

"More of you?" she giggled. "Well, not *more.* I want you to take me. Hard."

I chuckled. This one was a minx in the bedroom. I *loved* it.

I slowly slid out of her and thrust back in. Hard.

She cried out. As I slammed into her again, I watched her face twist in ecstasy. She was suddenly breathing hard. I pulled out and thrust into her again, faster, harder. She moaned and cried out as I fucked her, my hips slapping against her thighs. Her breasts bounced up and down as I pounded into her. Her body was small, tight, but she grew accustomed to my size. The feeling of her around my cock was *fantastic.*

She started moaning, her voice filling the room and accentuating the sounds of our bodies against each other.

She was getting closer to orgasm.

I watched her face as her brows knit together and her

mouth rounded in an O as she moaned. She grabbed onto my shoulders, her fingers digging into my skin, and a moment later she cried out, her body convulsing and curling around mine. She moaned loudly, and her face was the sexiest thing I'd ever seen.

For a moment, she was breathless, her pussy contracting around my cock.

When she fell back onto the couch, she gasped and panted.

"Holy shit," she said, breathless.

"Yeah," I said.

She tapped my hip. I frowned and pulled out of her. She turned around to kneel on the couch, her hands on the back. She looked at me over her shoulder.

"It's your turn," she said, that same smile I'd been lusting after all night playing on her lips.

She didn't have to ask me twice. I stood behind her and grabbed her hips. When I pushed into her, her round ass cheeks were cushions against my thighs. The view of her ass narrowing into her waist, her strawberry blond hair on her shoulders and back, was enough of a sight to bring a man to his knees.

I started pumping into her again. My cock slid in and out of her, and she moaned loudly with every stroke. I fucked her harder and harder. Her breasts swung back and forth. I reached around her and grabbed onto one, pulling her back against me. Her back was arched, ass pointing out, chest up. I pushed my fingers into her hair and kissed her neck, her cheek. She turned her face, and I kissed her on the lips twice before I released her back to the couch.

She held on as I grabbed her hips again. I fucked her as if the world was coming to an end and this was the last time we would ever get to fuck. She moaned and cried out, and I could feel the orgasm building. My balls tightened and my cock hardened inside of her. Any moment now, I was going to release.

I gasped louder and louder.

"Come for me, baby," she said, looking over her shoulder.

And again, I didn't let her ask me twice.

I groaned, shoving my cock into her as deep as I could, pumping my load into her. She cried out, and I realized she was orgasming, too, her pussy contracting around my cock in the same rhythm as before.

It felt like it lasted forever.

When we finally came down, she collapsed over the back of the couch, head hanging down. I pulled out of her and sat down next to her, breathing hard. My wrapped-up cock glistened with her juices. Her thighs were slick from my sweat, and it was hot, hot, hot.

She sank onto the cushions next to me.

"That was incredible," she said.

I chuckled through my heavy breathing. "You're just saying that to stroke my ego."

"Honey, we've already stroked everything else."

I laughed, shaking my head. "You're something else, Piper."

She leaned over and kissed my cheek.

"I should probably get going," I said. I rolled the condom off my cock. She stood, walked a few steps, leaned around a doorway, and brought back a wastebasket for me to discard the aftermath of our sex.

"Thanks for coming." She grinned at her joke.

"Any time," I added with a wink.

So fucking cliché, but I loved how easygoing it was with her.

I stood.

She wasn't asking me to stay and cuddle. She wasn't taking offense that I wanted to leave. Everything was just *easy* with her. Simple. Comfortable.

It was a pity she was just passing through town.

I found my clothes in a trail on the floor and got dressed. She disappeared into the bedroom— so *that's* where it was— and appeared again wearing a large T-shirt. It almost covered her, but not quite. Her nipples were still hard and poking against the fabric.

She walked me to the door.

"In the business of making people happy, huh?" she asked, and I remembered I'd said that stupid line. Why couldn't I have said anything else?

Smooth move, Ethan.

"Well, you certainly did your job tonight," she said.

She smiled at me and paused. I knew I had work in the morning, but I couldn't resist. I reached for her, pulling her close to me and pressing my mouth against hers. She gasped.

"Hard again already?" she murmured, reaching for my cock.

I pulled the T-shirt over her head and moved my mouth to her full breast, sucking on her nipple.

"For you, I am," I said.

"Then let's see what we can do about that," she said as she unbuckled my belt.

TWO

PIPER

I opened my eyes and looked up at the ceiling that wasn't familiar yet.

My apartment in Roanoke had been a lot smaller than this house was. I'd only been here in North Haven, Virginia, for two nights, but so far, I liked it.

Not to mention the company this place kept.

I smiled when I thought of Ethan and the way he'd touched me. Kissed me. Fucked me.

I curled under the sheets, raw between my legs. I flashed on him hovering over me, hips thrusting, his hand on my breast when he'd come from behind. Then, in our second go-around, when he'd gone down on me and made me come three more times. We'd gone at it for hours before he finally went home, saying he had to work early.

God, I hadn't had sex like that in a long time. Hot. Delicious. *Mind-blowing.*

In the business of making people happy.

I hadn't asked him what he meant by that, what it was he did. We'd had our little game, where we'd been cryptic enough to keep it interesting. And it had gotten real enough for me to want something like that again.

I wasn't going to date any time soon, though. My ex-boyfriend, Chris, had needed a mother, not a girlfriend, and I was done being tied down, thank you very much.

The feeling of euphoria slowly faded as I sat up and shook off the dregs of the fantasy I'd lived last night.

I'd *slept* with someone. A one-night stand in the true sense of the word.

I *never* had one-night stands. It was so unlike me. But he'd been so *hot*. And charming. And funny. And I'd been tipsy, which had lowered my inhibitions.

God, alcohol was a demon.

I'd gotten carried away, and now here I was, the morning after, feeling the glow of the sexual aftermath. And a twisting stomach because I'd done something I wasn't sure I was okay with.

It had been a hell of a lot of fun, though. And I wanted to start being fun. Chris had always told me to just relax.

Don't get your panties in a twist, babe. Why can't you just take a chill pill? You always have a stick up your ass.

My life here in North Haven was a new chapter. And along with it came a new me. It was good that I let the walls come down.

Besides, I wasn't ever going to see the guy again. He had a fancy Land Rover. He was probably a rich businessman or something, always on the road.

I definitely wasn't going to start sleeping around. It was just a one-time thing.

My alarm buzzed on my nightstand, and I switched it off, walking to the shower. I pulled the large shirt I'd slept in over my head and stepped under the spray. The smell of our sex last night filled the shower cubicle again, even though

I'd cleaned up last night, and I felt his touch on my skin again.

I didn't have time to stand in the shower and dream. It was my first day at North Haven Hospital, and I had to get my ass in gear if I didn't want to be late. Nurses couldn't be late. We were the backbone of the hospital. I'd set my alarm for much later than usual since I'd been up until the wee hours drinking and frolicking with a stranger.

I hadn't had a chance to call my mom since I'd moved into my new house. I'd hoped to chat with my parents before I started, but that would have to wait until after.

I'd only been in town for two days, and I already missed my family back in Roanoke. Leaving hadn't been easy, but it had been time to make a change. If I hadn't left, I'd be back in Chris's arms right now, pathetic enough to take him back when what I needed to do was leave him behind.

The job opportunity at North Haven Hospital had been a godsend. And the money wasn't bad, either. I was excited to learn from one Dr. Cole, who I'd heard was among the best in southern Virginia. Three damn good reasons to leave home, in other words.

It was time for my adventure to begin.

Charlie meowed and crawled out from under the bed.

"Oh, good morning, baby," I cooed and scooped him up when he rubbed himself against my legs. "Where were you all night? I missed you."

Charlie purred when I scratched him behind the ears. He was the one thing I'd been able to bring from home. I'd had my Bengal cat since graduation, and he always made me laugh. Animals were a gift to mankind, and no one could tell me differently.

He must have hidden while Ethan had been here,

though. The poor little guy was struggling to adjust to the move. He'd barely set a paw outside his hiding place yet.

"We'll figure it out, you and me," I said, planting kisses on his head. He squeezed his eyes shut as I scratched him. "Before we know it, this will be home."

I set him down on the bed. "I have to go to work. Be back later."

I left the house and drove to the hospital, pulling into staff parking. After signing some forms and getting my badge from human resources, I reported to the head emergency room nurse to handle more paperwork before I was allowed to settle in.

The head nurse, Susan, was a stately older woman who looked like tradition and rules kept her going. After our meeting, the door opened.

"This is Adriana," Susan said. "She'll show you the ropes."

I smiled at the nurse who'd come in.

"Piper Edwards," I said.

"Come on," she said, nodding her head. "I'll show you where we nap when the doctors aren't looking." She giggled. "Joking," she said to Susan, who seemed to hide a smile.

I followed Adriana out. She was already talking, but I'd missed the start of her conversation. She was shorter than I was by half a head with her jet-black hair pulled into a ponytail. Her brown eyes were friendly, and her chatter was instantly endearing.

"This ER is like a family, you know? It can be stressful sometimes, but we nurses look out for each other. It's the same all over in this little town. Everyone knows everyone here."

"I prefer it that way," I said. "In Roanoke, I felt like just another number. I think I'll love living in a small town."

"Well, we'll see how much you love it when everyone knows all about your business because they're so nosy."

She grinned at me over her shoulder.

"Supply closet," she said, pushing the door open to a room with shelves everywhere.

"Locker room," she said, pushing open another.

"That's the restroom."

I followed her through the hospital as we left the ER area.

"And finally, this is the cafeteria," she said. "The most important place in this whole hospital."

I laughed. "Noted."

"Trust me, this will become your haven. You know how our lives are as nurses. Coffee will pull you through the long hours of the night. And their cakes will get you through most of the crazy shit we see around here. They have a seat with my name on it over there."

"Really?"

She shook her head. "No, but they should."

I laughed. I liked Adriana. She was quirky and funny. And she didn't treat me like I was a stranger just because I was new here.

"So, now for the rules. You're allowed to sleep with other nurses. But not the doctors."

"Hospital policy?"

She shook her head. "No, not technically. We just don't. They don't look at us that way. They're gods. We're mere mortals."

I giggled. "Seriously?"

"Besides," she continued, "it has to be taken to HR if you do decide to get involved with someone. But it's gossip-worthy and everyone will be all over it. Scandals and gossip are our only true form of entertainment around here."

"Oh, don't you worry," I said. "I don't intend on getting involved with anyone."

"No? Not even dating?"

I shook my head. "I just went through the breakup from hell. Which is exactly why I'm not interested."

"You need to tell me what happened there," Adriana said.

And I figured I probably would, eventually. I could see myself being friends with her.

"I'm serious about sleeping with doctors," she said. "Trust me, you'll want to. Some of them are as hot as hell. It's a crime to make the people you're supposed to save lives with so hot you can't think straight. But you'll build an immune system as we did."

"We?"

Just as I asked, a male nurse came down the corridor and joined us.

"Oh, fresh meat," he said.

His blond hair was combed to the side, and his skin was *perfect*. He was tall and skinny and looked me up and down the way a woman did when she thought I was competition.

"This is Jeremy," Adriana said. "Meet Piper. She won't steal your guys; she's off 'em for now."

"Guys?" I asked.

Adriana nodded. "Jeremy isn't out to everyone, so hush about it. But you trust us, don't you, honey?"

"Sure," Jeremy said, frowning at me a little. "Until proven otherwise."

I smiled at him. "Your secret is safe with me. And your guys are safe, too."

Jeremy's smile broadened. "I think we'll get along just

fine. I trust Adriana's judgment." He looped his arm through mine. "Did you see the doctors yet?"

"I hear they're gorgeous."

"*Delish.* But they don't look at *us.*" He sighed. "Such a pity. But we march on, save lives, and stay in our league."

I giggled.

"Oh, we noble martyrs," Adriana said and pressed the back of her hand against her forehead. "Come on, I'll get you started on Mrs. Kaufman. She's a pain, so we get her out of the way first. After that, it's smooth sailing."

"I have to split, I have Mr. Keller," Jeremy said. "I'll see you around, Pipes." The nickname was endearing coming from him. "I'm sure you'll have a lot of fun here."

I nodded. I was pretty sure I was going to have fun here, too.

THREE

ETHAN

"Good morning, Mr. Keller," I said, walking into the elderly man's room.

He had come into the ER with a bout of asthma that had been particularly bad. Once we stabilized him, he was transferred to the intensive care unit, which meant he was still my patient. In a tiny hospital like North Haven's, we often had to take care of ICU patients as well. "How are we feeling today?"

"As useless as always," Keller huffed. "I can't do anything when I'm tied to these confounded beds."

"No one is tying you down, but it is for your safety that we keep you for at least one more night." I took his chart from the foot of the bed. "Has your dizziness returned at all?"

Keller muttered something inaudible, and I leaned in a little to hear what he was saying. The old man grumbled a lot. He wasn't my favorite patient, but I understood him. Getting old had to be a bitch. Slowly losing control, going from being independent and strong to gradually needing others more and more had to be hard.

I was independent as hell and liked to keep it that way. The idea of getting old... well, best not think about something that wasn't going to happen any time soon.

"And you should tell your nurses to budge on the dessert portions, too," Keller was saying, complaining about the hospital food.

"If it's any consolation," I said with a chuckle, "no one is perfectly happy with hospital food."

Keller grumbled again. Nurses scuffled back and forth past the room door, doing their duties. I was aware of their movement, seeing it from the corner of my eye. I didn't know what prompted me to look up when a flash of blonde passed in my field of vision. There were a lot of blonde nurses. But none of them were quite like *her*.

She was gone before I could be sure.

"Will you excuse me, Mr. Keller?" I said and walked to the door, popping my head around the frame.

Yes, there she was. Piper. Talking to one of my nurses. And wearing *scrubs*.

She *was* one of my nurses.

What the hell?

She wore the ID tag the new nurses were issued to show that they weren't completely up to scratch just yet and the rest of us had to pitch in with answers when they needed guidance.

I'm in the business of picking up the slack.

God, there would have been no way to guess that was what she'd meant. But my answer had been just as mysterious. It had been fun and games at the bar last night, hadn't it? We were messing around, flirting, being cute.

Now, I wished I'd asked her what she did more directly. I'd assumed she was only passing through.

Now, I *wished* she'd only been passing through. God, I

didn't sleep with anyone at work. Personal policy. It was unprofessional, and it distracted from saving lives, which was why I was here.

With her working in my ER, I'd broken my own rule without knowing it. And that downright pissed me off.

I really should have been more diligent about finding out who she was. But I hadn't recognized her, and in a town as small as North Haven, not knowing them usually meant they were tourists. I knew all the locals.

My mistake. A big one.

I could stay away from her, right? I could do something else, keep myself busy with my rounds, hide out in my office...

Pathetic.

I wasn't going to let this become a problem, though.

"I said, what are you gawking at?"

Mr. Keller was calling to me from his bed, and I sighed, turning around to look at him. He looked small and frail between the thick pillows and sheets, his skin wrinkled with barely any hair left on his head. But his personality was larger than life, and his arms were crossed over his chest, making him look demanding and grumpy.

"I just had to make sure my nurses are taken care of. I'll come to see you again later, Mr. Keller, and we'll see if you'll be ready to go home in the morning."

"I'm ready to go home now," he huffed.

I smiled politely. "I'll see you later."

I left the room, glancing in the direction I'd seen Piper. She was gone, though.

I turned in the other direction, heading to my next patient, and hoped I wasn't going to run into her.

After seeing to my patients, I called the staff together for a quick meeting. When they were all collected in front of me in the staff room, I looked around at the faces before me. Some of them looked exhausted, with dark circles beneath their eyes and sallow cheeks. Others looked fresh, having just arrived to take over for some of the other shifts. The shifts could be grueling, lasting twelve hours each, but it was part of the job.

The moment we chose to become health care providers, we knew we'd be sacrificing many nights of sleep.

It was an occupational hazard.

"I get that you're tired," I said sternly. "But the charts haven't been updated correctly, and I don't appreciate it. I'm not just talking about the interns, either." I glanced at the interns, who looked exhausted and scared to be here. They were at the start of their year, and they were still terrified of anyone in control. It would lessen as they got to know everyone they worked with, but they would learn to never lose their fear of me.

"All the information is there, though, right?" one of the interns asked.

I glared at him. He was short, dark-haired, and reminded me of a deer caught in headlights.

"What's your point?"

"Well... *isn't* that the point? That the information is there to be able to take care of people? Even if it's not done exactly right—"

"Do you think this is a joke?" I snapped, interrupting him. "This isn't med school, where you get to guess what questions you might be asked and hope for a pass. If you don't do it right here, people die. And trust me, that's not something you want on your conscience. If you could have prevented it, you will beat yourself up about it for months, maybe years, depending on how badly you screwed up."

They all stared at me with big eyes and clenched jaws.

"Get out of my sight," I said, looking away from them as if in disgust. "I know you'll do better. We expect it from you. Your patients deserve it. And you owe it to yourselves."

They dispersed. When they were almost all gone, filtering out of the room to return to their duties, Dr. Nathan Henson walked up to me. He was head of the oncology department and the only person who wasn't scared of me. We were friends, in fact. Apparently, he'd listened in on the tail end of the meeting.

"You shouldn't be so hard on them," he said, sitting on the edge of one of the tables and swinging his legs.

"Come on, Nate," I said. "You know how it goes. This isn't a game."

Nate nodded. "Yeah, I know. But they're giving it their all. Don't you remember what it was like when you just started?"

I sighed. "Yeah, I do. I remember having a hell of a lot more on my plate than most of these kids do. And I still got my charts right."

Nate chuckled. "They don't call you the bulldog for nothing."

"Is that what they call me?" I asked, rubbing my face.

"Don't tell me you didn't know."

"I heard a rumor, but I try to ignore those."

Nate chuckled again. "I guess you consider them to be distractions?"

"I consider them to be not worth my time."

Nate understood where I was coming from, although he couldn't relate. He was laidback and relaxed, which was incredible considering his department had the highest mortality rate in the hospital. But he could distance himself from his work and not get emotionally involved the way I did.

"Everyone already respects you for your reputation," Nate spoke again. "You don't have to make them fear you, too."

"It's how I do things. It's how I've always done things."

Nate pulled up his shoulders. "Just try to speak to them the way you would have liked your superiors to talk to you."

I glanced at Nate. "They'll get used to me. They always do."

Nate laughed. "Yeah, they have no choice."

I shrugged one shoulder and checked my phone.

"I have to get going," I said. "I have a few things I need to do to get my admin caught up before I do more rounds."

"I have to check in with a few people, too. I'll see you at lunch?"

"Sure," I said.

Nate left the staff room, whistling, with his hands in his pockets. He was the popular doctor. They all liked him. But he was a likable guy. We each had our talents.

Mine happened to be jumping into the fray and saving lives against all odds.

I retreated to my office and tried to focus on my work. By the time I got through all the paperwork, it was time for my rounds again. I left the room to find three nurses standing outside my office waiting for me. One of whom was Piper.

Her eyes widened when she saw me and slid down my body and back up, taking in the stethoscope around my neck and the white doctor's coat. She swallowed hard.

God, whose idea had this been? Why was she on my rounds? Was this some sick cosmic joke? The universe reminding me that I'd screwed up?

"Ready?" I asked them without missing a beat.

The others mumbled confirmation. Piper didn't speak.

As we walked down the corridor, I was hyperaware of Piper behind me. We stepped into the first room, and my mind was too focused on her.

"How are you, Miss Ferguson?" I asked the young redhead who sat up in bed, a glazed look in her eyes whenever I walked into the room.

I started running through the usual questions, but I wasn't thinking about Miss Ferguson and her injuries after an accident. My attention drifted to Piper where she stood in the corner of the room, observing, since this was clearly her first day.

She looked incredible in her scrubs, like a real-life fantasy, her blonde hair braided and the light blue scrubs making her green eyes only seem brighter.

I flashed on the memory of her face when she'd orgasmed beneath me, her mouth stretched in a silent O. I flashed on her breasts, skin like milk, nipples dark. My cock twitched in my pants.

"...what do you think, doctor?"

Miss Ferguson had been talking to me, and I hadn't heard a thing.

"Run that by me one more time," I said apologetically, kicking myself for getting distracted.

This was exactly what shouldn't have happened.

I couldn't have her here with me. Precisely because I wanted her.

FOUR

PIPER

Oh. My. God. Not only did Ethan work at the hospital, but he was also my boss. Yeah, the worst thing in the history of one-night stands had happened to me.

And since there were two other nurses on my shift, I had to act like everything was fine and dandy. Like we hadn't had mind-blowing sex since I'd thought he was just passing through. Like I hadn't brought him to my *home* thinking it didn't matter if he knew where I lived.

Could things be any worse?

Well, they could.

Because as polite as Ethan was to the patients—and judging by their reaction to him, he was a good doctor, loved by all he treated—he treated his staff like pure shit.

When Nicky, one of the other nurses with me, dropped a syringe, he glared at her and asked if she understood the germ theory of disease. Tina, the third nurse on our little rotation, had forgotten which vial was the right one when Ethan had asked her to add it to the IV. As soon as we'd left the room, he'd snapped at her that she had better study a little more because mistakes like that could cost lives.

He'd been right in both instances, of course. Ethan hadn't been *wrong*. But he'd been rude about it. It hadn't been necessary to be so hard on the staff when, honestly, they were doing their best. And I was sure that they wouldn't have made any mistakes if Ethan hadn't made them so nervous.

The only reason he hadn't let me have it, too, was because I was just observing today, making sure that I knew everything that needed to happen before I was in charge of doing it.

I couldn't believe Ethan was *the* Dr. Cole, the best ER doctor in southern Virginia. I'd been so eager to learn from him.

Now, I felt utterly disappointed.

Sure, he'd been funny and charming and attractive last night. And the sex had been amazing. Beyond amazing.

But that didn't make up for him being an ass to people. He was cocky, arrogant, so full of himself there was hardly space for anyone else when his ego joined him in a room.

God, it was embarrassing, to say the least.

The patients loved him, but that wasn't what made a hospital good. What made a hospital good was how the staff worked together, how well they got along, how they worked as a unit.

There was no guessing where Ethan imagined himself to be on the food chain.

And I was less than impressed.

Patient care was about *care*. Not just for the patients, but for those who were responsible for their lives, too.

Ethan was an asshole.

First impressions were one thing, but having seen him now, it was safe to say that I couldn't stand him.

Not. One. Bit.

"Nurse Edwards," Ethan called me where I leaned against the wall, trying to get my emotions under control. "Can I see you for a moment?"

I wanted to say no, but he was my boss.

I nodded and followed him away from the other nurses, away from where anyone could see us. When he walked into the supply close—a supply closet? Really—and closed the door behind me, I dropped my submissive act and glared at him.

"This isn't quite what I expected," he said.

"Yeah, me neither."

"We aren't going to be able to avoid each other, that much is clear," he said.

I'd thought about that, too. The hospital wasn't that big. And we were on the same damn rotation.

"We're just going to have to learn to work together," he added.

"Right." I was sullen.

"And under no circumstances can you mention what happened between us last night to anyone. I expect you to remain professional at all times."

I gaped at him, not knowing what to say. I hadn't expected him to bring up the sex. At least, not like that.

"What makes you think I want to talk about it at all?" I asked.

He blinked at me.

"It's not like it was something to write home about, you know." I was lying through my teeth.

"Wasn't it?" he asked.

Something about his voice sounded a little deeper, a little gruffer than a moment ago, and I was suddenly aware of how close we were to each other in the closet, forced together in a space that was far too small for two people. Could he not have chosen somewhere else to lecture me? His cologne was in my nostrils. I swallowed hard. He was close enough to touch. He was close enough to press myself up against.

Stop it, I scolded myself.

"No," I said, but my voice was breathy, and I didn't sound nearly as convincing as I'd hoped.

"Well, now that we both agree," he said, and it was like he was shutting himself down again, distancing himself from me. How did he do that? How could he just recover when I was left breathless and reeling?

"Now that that's taken care of," he rephrased curtly and opened the door, stepping out with authority and confidence.

I stayed behind, trying to pull myself together again. When I was ready, I popped my head out of the closet to see if the coast was clear before I stepped out, too.

I felt unbalanced. I'd been set on disliking him, but it was impossible as soon as we were in close confines together.

Dammit.

"Where have you been?" Adriana asked when she finally found me.

"Admin with the director," I lied. "More paperwork for my paycheck since I'm new."

Adriana bought it and looped her arm through mine.

"We're meeting Jeremy in the cafeteria. He should have plenty of gossip for us to sink our teeth into by now. You'll love the stories that go around here."

I nodded and forced a smile. I was just going to have to make sure none of those stories were about me and Ethan.

By the time I clocked out and headed home, I felt torn.

Other than Ethan's surprise appearance in the ER, I had a good feeling about the hospital so far. And moving to North Haven had been the best thing I'd done. Getting away from Chris and his toxicity had changed everything for me.

But I wanted to go home. I wanted to see my mom, to cry on her shoulder about what had happened. I wanted to ask for her advice.

What was I supposed to do? Was I going to stick it out at the hospital because I couldn't let a one-night stand ruin a potentially great career for me? Or was I going to tuck my tail between my legs and run back home because this was trouble, and I didn't know if I was capable of handling it? Maybe I could ask if I could be moved to a different department.

My first day had been hard work. It was a strain to work at the hospital. Not only because Ethan was there, but because I was new. I had a lot to learn and very little time to do it all in.

Ethan was just the cherry on top of a very crappy combination.

I walked into the house and Charlie ran to me, rubbing his spotted fur up against my legs.

"Hey, big guy," I said, scooping him up in my arms and nuzzling his neck. He squeezed his eyes shut and purred. He always made me feel better. I was so glad I hadn't come all this way alone. "Did you miss me?"

He continued purring as I carried him to the living room. I dumped my bag on the floor and collapsed on the couch with Charlie curled up against my chest.

"You won't believe what happened."

I scratched him between the ears and decided not to call my mom. I was a big girl. I could deal with this. It wasn't the end of the world, and if I ran back to my mom every time something went wrong, I wasn't going to learn to deal with my life on my own.

"Come on," I said, setting Charlie on the floor. "Let's get busy."

I showered, getting rid of the hospital smell that somehow clung to my skin even after I'd tried to scrub it off, and walked into the spare bedroom where I'd dumped most of my boxes. I found a boxcutters and opened them one by one, walking through the house, decorating, and setting things up.

Creating a home.

Pictures on the fireplace mantle, fake plants in the corners to spice up the room. Real plants died when I had double shifts, but artificial plants still made it seem like I could keep my life together.

I found pictures of my parents, my friends back home, and scenes from last Christmas. A wave of homesickness washed over me.

It hadn't been easy to break away. I'd hoped that moving here and getting to know the town and people would allow me to forget about everything I'd left behind.

But it wasn't going to be that easy, was it?

At the bottom of a box, I found a jewelry bag, black velvet, held shut by a drawstring. When I opened it, the rings and necklaces and bracelets Chris had given me throughout our relationship spilled into my palm.

I sat down on the bed, pulled up my legs, and sighed, looking down at the pile of memories that had somehow made it into the box.

Charlie moved, curling up against me. I absently scratched him.

"So, even Chris managed to come along, somehow," I said to Charlie. "If he had just picked himself up from the couch and done something, maybe he could have been here for real. But he had to sacrifice it all for the sake of *comfort*."

My eyes stung with tears, but I swallowed down the lump that grew in my throat. I wasn't going to cry about that sad sack of a man. He was pathetic, and he didn't deserve my tears.

Even though we'd been together for the longest time. Even though I'd sacrificed so much for him. I'd given him so many good years of my life. I'd worked my fingers to the bone to support us when he'd decided to quit his job because it wasn't quite "the right fit" for him and then he didn't bother finding another.

"No," I said sternly. "We're not going to think about him, right?"

Charlie made a small meowing sound, answering me when I spoke to him.

"Right. We're going to look forward, not back." I sighed. "Even if the way forward also contains an asshole now."

I chuckled. It was ironic. Who would have thought that breaking out of my usual mold, doing something different, would come back to bite me in the ass like that?

I tipped the jewelry back into the velvet bag and lay back onto the bed, closing my eyes. For the first time, I didn't feel the need to text or call Chris, I realized. That was something, wasn't it? I'd always felt like I couldn't live without him. But this time, I felt like I could. I could leave him behind if I had to. Yeah, so it hurt. But it wasn't impossible.

The move to North Haven, however bumpy a start I'd gotten off to, had been the right move. This was proof.

I sat up and looked at Charlie.

"We're going to do this, you and me."

He purred again, rolling onto his back and stretching out on the bed.

I giggled and got up, ready to unpack another box.

FIVE

PIPER

When I woke up the next morning, I felt better about everything. I headed to the hospital and got to work, focusing on my job rather than on the one-night stand that turned out to be my boss.

Yesterday, I'd been tired and overwhelmed by my first day. I'd been emotional and homesick. But with a new day came new courage. I could do this

I just had to stop thinking about Ethan at all and do what I had come here to do.

Make people feel better.

"Good morning, Mrs. Kaufman," I said to the middle-aged woman in the ICU everyone dreaded to see first thing.

I didn't think she was that bad. I wasn't sure why everyone was so weary of her.

I waited until she'd opened her eyes and adjusted to the fact that it was a new day before I flicked on the lights. It was still early, and the patients I had to see were mostly still asleep.

"Why do you have to do your rounds so early?" Mrs. Kaufman asked. "I would love to sleep in just once."

"If all goes well, you can go home soon. Then you can sleep in all you like." I checked her charts and started preparing her meds.

"Sometimes I feel like I'm going to be stuck here forever."

"I don't think so. You're showing significant progress." I prepared the syringe and administered the medication. I rubbed the spot on her arm where I'd jabbed her and smiled.

I'd realized very early on in my career that the patients were more scared than anything else. They didn't know what was wrong, the doctors didn't always tell them everything they needed to know, and they were in shock after being poked and prodded so many times. A lot of the patients became snappy as a defense mechanism. It was a typical fight-or-flight response.

A kind word, a smile, and a bit of reassurance always went a long way.

It was no different with Mrs. Kaufman. I'd learned to treat the patients as I would treat my friends and family. And things got better.

"How are you settling in?" Mrs. Kaufman asked, finger-combing her bottle-blonde hair. I'd told her yesterday that I'd come from Roanoke and that I was nervous. The moment she'd realized I was as unsure as she was, she'd eased up a little.

"Much better today," I said. "It just takes time. A person can get used to anything if you take it one day at a time."

"It's so true," Mrs. Kaufman said. "I'm getting used to that chemical smell that's everywhere, for instance. I can't wait to get back home."

"Soon," I said and smiled.

I made sure she had everything she needed before I headed on to my next patient.

In the corridor, I ran into Adriana, who looked half asleep. She yawned before she smiled at me.

"Good morning, sunshine," she said. "Second day already, huh?"

I nodded. "It's going to be a good one, too."

Adriana chuckled. "That's the spirit. You look very... awake."

"I'm a morning person," I said.

She laughed. "I'm not. I prefer working night shift."

We were all on rotation, doing different shifts throughout the month. I preferred night shift too, although it messed with my sleep pattern. There was just something about being there for those so vulnerable when the rest of the world was asleep.

"What are you doing after work?" Adriana asked.

"I don't have any plans yet."

"So, come out with us," Adriana offered. "Jeremy and I are going to our favorite bar, the Howling Wolf, to have a couple of drinks and let our hair down."

I giggled when I imagined Jeremy letting his hair down. He was a character, all right.

"What do you say?" Adriana asked.

I nodded. "Sure, why not?"

"That's the spirit." She flipped her dark hair over her shoulder. "Gotta go get these rounds done. The doctors get pissed off when we don't do our jobs before they come through for their rounds."

I thought about Ethan and fought the urge to roll my eyes. I'd seen how he'd treated the staff yesterday when things weren't just the way he wanted it. I could just imagine the poor nurses he'd have a problem with.

I realized I was thinking about Ethan when I'd resolved not to and firmly pushed the thought of him aside. I had a job to do, and later, I was going to have a good time with my friends. That was all there was to it.

"Mr. Keller," I said, walking into the old man's room. He was already up and glaring at me.

"The new girl," he grumbled.

"How are you feeling today?"

"Fine. I want to go home."

"Dr. Cole will be around shortly, and then I'm sure he'll sign off on it."

"The doctors all find an excuse to keep me here. It's a damn money-making scheme, if you ask me."

I smiled and shook my head. "We're just looking out for your well-being, Mr. Keller. As soon as we know you'll be okay once you leave, we want you to go home and enjoy your life."

Mr. Keller huffed, but a smile played around his lips while I made sure he had everything he needed. He was a grumpy old man, rumored to be a pain in the ass, but I liked elderly people like Mr. Keller. Life through their eyes had to be so very different than my own perspective.

By the time lunch rolled around, Adriana and I walked to the cafeteria together. She pushed open the door and stepped through. Just as I followed, Ethan came barging out of the cafeteria, nearly running me over.

I tripped and almost fell, but he grabbed my arm, saving me from going down.

For a moment, our eyes locked, and something electric passed between us.

"Thank you," I breathed.

"Watch where you're going," he snapped. "Nurses

aren't supposed to be underfoot. We have enough to deal with as it is."

I blinked wide eyes at him, so surprised by his outburst that I couldn't find the words. He marched away from me, and the cafeteria door swung shut.

"Well, that was cute," Adriana said sarcastically. "You should be glad he caught you at all."

"Yeah, I imagined he would just let me fall."

"He's so rude," Adriana said. "A hell of a good doctor. And hot. But God, moody like a woman."

"I'm a woman, and I never act like that," I protested.

"Yeah, but honey, you're nice."

I giggled as we walked to the queue that snaked around the display counters with the food.

My mind was on Ethan as I stared at the sandwiches, barely seeing them. He'd been just as rude to me as the day before. But I had felt something when he touched me, something electric... *No*. It was the right thing to do to stay professional—and as far away from him as possible.

The rest of the day was uneventful. I wasn't put on Ethan's rounds again—thank God—and despite being in the same department, I didn't see him.

I knocked off work, headed home, showered, and dressed in jeans and a cute T-shirt. Adriana picked me up, and we drove to the Howling Wolf together.

The bar was louder than The Tavern, where I'd met Ethan, and more crowded. Everywhere, groups of people sat around tables with drinks in front of them, talking and laughing.

Jeremy waved at us from a table at the side, and we made our way to him.

"What took you so long?" he asked when we both sat

down. "If I'd come with you guys, we wouldn't have found a table."

"You're a saint," Adriana said. "I'll buy you a drink."

Jeremy smiled, happy with what he was getting out of it, and looked around.

"A lot of talent around here tonight," he said, eyeing three guys who stood at the bar.

"Oh, they're cute," Adriana said.

I laughed and shook my head. I wasn't going to join in ogling everyone. I wasn't interested in dating, and after what had happened with Ethan, I was cured from wanting a one-night stand. Instead, I took Adriana and Jeremy's orders and walked to the bar. We'd settled on three margaritas.

I looked around while I waited for our drinks. The atmosphere was great. I liked it here.

"Hey, beautiful," someone said next to me. I turned and looked at a guy who leaned against the bar, swaying a little.

"I'm here with someone," I said politely.

"Oh, come on, darlin'. Let me buy you a drink."

I giggled. "Noble, but I already paid. Thanks."

The bartender brought my drinks, and I carried them to our table, getting away from my new suitor.

"What was that?" Adriana asked.

"Someone who wanted to pay for the drinks."

"You should have let him," Adriana said.

"Oh, no," Jeremy said, shaking his head. "Not unless she was willing to give him something in return. Like her number or her virtue."

I laughed. "Who calls it that anymore?"

Jeremy shrugged. "Your body is a temple. It's sacred."

"Don't get me started on sacred," Adriana said. "Nothing you do is sacred."

Jeremy sniffed. "Well, I wouldn't hesitate to let

someone pay for my drinks, but then again, I have a lot to give."

Adriana collapsed in a fit of giggles, and I laughed, sipping my cocktail.

"This place is nice," I said. "And best of all, I don't see anyone from work."

"Yeah, this isn't a hospital hangout," Adriana said. "Which is why we come here. It's good to escape sometimes. Especially the doctors. So, rest assured, you're not going to see Dr. Cole here tonight."

I'd been searching for him through the crowd, I realized. And I felt relief when Adriana said it.

"Why wouldn't you want to see Dr. Cole?" Jeremy asked.

"Because he was an ass to her today," Adriana answered for me.

"A hot ass," Jeremy said. "I could look at that backside all day."

Adriana and I both burst out laughing.

"Yeah, keep it in your pants," Adriana said, still giggling. She told Jeremy what had happened.

"It could've been a cute moment, like in the movies. But only if he weren't so rude," Jeremy said.

I nodded. It would have been a perfectly wonderful moment if he'd just been a human being about it.

"That's the thing with Dr. Cole, though," Jeremy said. "He's so serious about his job, it makes him cranky. He never has any fun. I don't think he even gets laid."

Oh, God. I knew for a fact that he got laid. And that he had a lot of fun when he wasn't at the hospital. Just thinking about our night together got me all hot and bothered. That night together had been *incredible*. But good sex didn't make up for how he'd treated me.

I brought my icy glass up to my cheek to cool my face off, worried I was turning red.

And I wasn't going to mention anything about the other night to Jeremy and Adriana. Sure, they would die to know. But Adriana had warned me that gossip was the main form of amusement, and when I listened to how these two talked about everyone, it was true. I couldn't afford for it to come out that Ethan and I had slept together.

I was just going to have to keep it from my new friends.

Someone stumbled over to our table, and I recognized the man from the bar.

"I told you I'm not interested," I said politely.

"Give me a chance. I bet I could rock your world."

"My world is in no need of rocking, thank you," I said.

Jeremy snorted and Adriana guffawed.

"Go on, she told you to get lost. She's nicer about it than I am," Adriana said when my new fan wouldn't leave. When he walked away, looking irritated that he'd struck out again, I shook my head.

"Are the guys all so overeager here?"

"God, I wish," Jeremy said.

"It's because you're new," Adriana offered. "And because you're beautiful, of course."

I started to protest, but she waved me off. "The locals want to eat you up," she said.

"Like I said, you're fresh meat," Jeremy said. "It's a little town, and it's not tourist season yet. People get a little bored of the same old faces."

"Well, good thing I'm not looking for anything. So many options, I wouldn't know where to start," I added sarcastically. Adriana and Jeremy burst out laughing again.

I smiled and sipped my cocktail, feeling more and more

at home. What more did anyone need than good friends and a good time?

I certainly didn't need a doctor who treated me like I was beneath him.

Even if my body was still craving his touch.

SIX

ETHAN

I couldn't get her off my mind, and it was driving me crazy. Just when I'd thought I'd gotten rid of any thoughts of her, I'd bumped into her, and it was just like those movies where sparks flew. Dammit, when I'd caught her from falling, I'd wanted to pull her close and kiss her.

Her green eyes had been bright, lips parted in shock when she'd nearly fallen and I'd caught her, and I'd wished we could be alone. She seemed to have that effect on me. Whenever I was around her, I wished the rest of the world would disappear.

But in the hospital, no one was ever alone. In a town as small as North Haven, someone was always looking. I had a reputation to uphold. I couldn't afford what had happened between us to get out. I couldn't afford gossip or rumors.

It was better if I stayed away from her completely.

But God, I wanted to do the opposite. I wanted to be all over her again. I wanted to hear her panting, her breath hot and heavy in my ear when I touched her, my hands between her legs. I wanted her wet and ready for me, her breasts and stomach flushed with the urge to have me inside of her.

Just thinking about it made my cock stiff in my pants. I shifted in my office chair, tugging at my belt, trying to make room for my erection.

I dropped my head into my hands. It was useless trying to focus on work when she was on my mind like this.

I marked the remainder of the paperwork to start with first thing in the morning, packed my things away, and locked my office. I walked through the hospital, nodding at the doctors passing me before I stepped out into the warmth of the setting sun.

My mind drifted to her again as I drove home—the swell of her breasts under my lips, her chest heaving. The feel of her against me when I moved between her legs.

The moans and cries that escaped her lips when I'd fucked her.

Fuck.

I was horny as hell. And there was nothing I could do about it. I didn't want to find someone random to get it out of my system. Not when Piper was the one on my mind. I had never minded having one-night stands—I'd preferred it. It was one thing sleeping with a stranger, though, and a different thing altogether to sleep with someone but think about someone else.

It just wouldn't do.

If this was the effect she had on me after we only bumped into each other, I was in trouble. She was in my department, which meant that I was going to run into her from time to time. It would be better if she was transferred to another department altogether.

But they would ask me why. I would have to give them a reason why I needed to get rid of her. And I didn't have a good explanation. She was good at her job, that much was certain. I didn't want her to get in trouble because I couldn't contain my lust.

And the ER needed nurses. We were always understaffed when something went wrong. And the ER was the one place everything always went wrong.

My patients would be upset when she didn't come around, too. I'd noticed she had a good bedside manner. She connected with the patients in a different way than the other nurses did. I had seen Mr. Keller this morning after I'd given him the all-clear to go home, how he had looked out for Piper and waved at her. Mr. Keller, the man who hated everyone in the hospital.

But not Piper.

No, I couldn't have her transferred. For a myriad of reasons.

It would be selfish of me to pluck her out of the ER and put her somewhere else just because I couldn't handle being around her. I was better than that, anyway.

I stopped at home, took my bag out of the car, and walked across the lawn to my front door. The house was bigger than what I needed as a loner. My brothers were all grown and didn't stay over anymore, but I liked to think that I had space for them if they needed me. Being the oldest of five meant I never seemed to grow out of being the responsible one.

"Ethan," a shaky voice called over the low wall separating my neighbor's place and mine. I smiled.

"How are you today, Viola?"

She smiled and shook her head. She was in her eighties, her white hair pulled back in a bun. She wore a wide-brimmed hat and sunglasses, even though the sun was starting to set.

"Don't use your doctor's voice on me, my boy. I see right through you."

I chuckled. "Force of habit. But I do want to know how you are."

"Oh, you know," she said, pulling up her narrow shoulders in a shrug. "Old age catches up with all of us eventually. How are things at the hospital?"

"Just great," I answered. I looked at her yard. The grass was long, and I knew she couldn't stand it. "Did Benjamin cancel on you again?"

She rolled her eyes. "His landscaping service has to be the worst in town."

"Let me set my things down and change, and then I'll mow it for you."

"Oh, I can't let you do that," she protested.

"It's no bother." I knew her blood pressure was high, and I didn't want her worrying about the grass.

"I know how busy you are, Ethan. I'm sure you don't have the time."

I smiled. "For you, I have all the time in the world."

Viola laughed and swatted gently at me. "Oh, you charmer. It's no wonder these nurses fall over their feet to get so much as a glimpse of you."

I laughed and shook my head, my thoughts drifting to Piper.

"They're not as fond of me as you imagine," I said.

"You're a star, Ethan. Thank you."

I walked inside my house, put my bag in the office, and walked to the bedroom, getting dressed in jeans and a T-shirt. I didn't mind doing Viola a favor now and then. She was a good neighbor, and my heart went out to her. Her husband had died a couple of years ago, and she was completely alone.

When I walked around to Viola's house, she had already taken out the lawnmower.

"You didn't have to do that. I would have gotten it," I said.

"I don't want you to do everything."

"Well, I've got this. Go inside, put your feet up, and I'll tell you when I'm done."

She reached for me and pinched my cheek with a smile before she walked into the house. I watched her shuffle along before I started the lawnmower and got to work.

When I was done, Viola had poured me a glass of lemonade. I thanked her for it, downed the contents of the glass, and excused myself.

"If there's anything I can do for you, you just let me know," Viola said.

"I will," I said, both of us knowing full well that I wasn't going to expect anything of her. She was getting old, and I considered it the duty of younger people to look after the elderly.

When I walked back home, it was almost dark. My house was cold and uninviting. I flicked on the lights as I went along, walking to the kitchen. Sometimes, I wished someone could be home waiting for me, someone who would make the place warmer, homier.

But that meant I would have to commit to a relationship of sorts, and I wasn't ready for that. So, the house was cold and quiet after I got home from work. So, what? Everything else in my life was exactly how I wanted it.

Irritated with myself for letting thoughts of Piper slip into my mind, I did a quick workout in my home gym. Usually, there was nothing like heavy weight on the bar to distract me, but it didn't work tonight. I kept thinking about her strawberry blonde hair, the smell of her skin... *Fuck.*

Hungry, I opened the fridge but couldn't find anything that looked enticing. I didn't feel like cooking.

Maybe getting takeout was a good idea. Generally, I tried to cook. It was healthier. If I fell into the rut of being a lazy bachelor, it was difficult to get out of. Just because I was single didn't mean that I had to be a slob.

But tonight, my mind was on Piper, and exceptions were fine.

I picked up the phone and ordered pizza.

I showered and then answered the door when the pizza arrived. I sat in front of the television, biting into the slices one by one as I tried to focus on the stupid comedy I was watching, desperately trying to force Piper out of my mind.

By the time the movie was finished, my eyes were gritty from exhaustion, and I was relieved.

Bedtime.

And as soon as I slept, Piper would disappear from my thoughts.

I walked to the bedroom, slid in between the sheets. I closed my eyes.

And flashed on images of Piper, her body delicate beneath mine.

Fuck.

I groaned and rubbed my eyes. My cock was hard in my boxers, begging for attention. Begging for release.

I wished Piper were here. God, the things I would do to her.

I pulled down my boxers and palmed my thick flesh. My cock was hot in my hand, and I pictured Piper again. I imagined kissing her, the taste of her lips on mine, her throaty moan when I slid my tongue into her mouth. Her mouth was warm, soft. Like I imagined her pussy would be. In my mind's eye, I spread her legs with my hands, fingers on the smooth skin of her thighs, her pussy wet and glistening, begging me to taste it. I envisioned closing my mouth around her, licking her clit, listening to her gasp and moan as I pushed her closer to the edge.

I pumped my hand up and down my cock, tugging and groaning as I pushed myself closer to an orgasm.

Her ass had been fucking *perfect* when I'd taken her from behind. I wanted to do it again. Push my hand into her hair, twist it around my fingers, and pull back, arching her back so that her breasts thrust outward while I thrust into her. I could hear her moans again, filling the room, the sound of our sex, my balls slapping against her pussy.

My hand pumped up and down my shaft like a piston, and I groaned when my release shot forward into the shirt I had ready. I collapsed as I caught my breath and then got up to throw the shirt in the washer.

Holy shit, I wanted her.

I wanted her so fucking badly.

SEVEN

ETHAN

Like the calm before a storm, things seemed to settle at the hospital again.

Realizing that Piper worked for me had come as a shock, and I had thought it would shake up life as I knew it.

But gradually, I got used to seeing her smoking hot body in my department.

I saw Piper in the corridors from time to time, and she had been on my rotation another three times. But we kept it professional. It wasn't different with her than with any of the other nurses. I was relieved about that.

The last thing I needed was for things to become complicated now that we worked together. Just because we had slept together that one time.

I was impressed that Piper was as professional about it as she was, too.

So what if sparks flew every time we were in a room together?

We were adults. We could restrain ourselves.

Relief, relief, relief.

And to think I had considered having her transferred to

another department. It had been premature. I'd been wise to wait and see how things would turn out.

Because they were perfectly fine now without me needing to take any kind of unnecessary action.

Things were quiet in the ER, too. Aside from a couple of minor emergencies, nothing really big had happened. But that always made me uneasy.

"So, things are going well, why question it?" Nate asked me when we sat in the cafeteria together. "You shouldn't jinx it, you know."

I shook my head, biting into my sandwich. "It's always like this. As soon as things calm down, I just know something bad is coming. It's like the eye of the hurricane. And the hurricane is always terrible."

Nate shook his head, chewing.

"That's the problem with you ER doctors. You always expect the worst. Sometimes, things are good without there being a reason for it."

I nodded, not willing to continue the argument. But I was getting anxious. It had been too long since something serious had happened. We hadn't had any critical patients, and we hadn't had ambulances squealing into the emergency bay with patients that clung to their lives, barely holding on.

North Haven's location nestled in steep mountains meant we saw more than our fair share of car accidents. Out-of-towners weren't used to the winding mountain roads and often miscalculated then ended up in our ER. And during tourist season, with alcohol-fueled festivities, the car accidents tripled.

Nate wouldn't understand, though. His job was slow-going. He saw patients, delivered the bad news, set them on programs for chemotherapy or radiation. Sometimes they made it, sometimes they didn't. The only villain in Nate's story was time itself. And it crept up on his patients, one way or another.

There was never a sense of urgency.

While I ate, my beeper went off. I grabbed it and looked at the screen.

"Here we go," I said, the feeling of dread settling in my stomach. "ER emergency. Better pray that I'm wrong."

Nate didn't have a chance to respond before I jumped up and ran out of the cafeteria.

I headed to the ER, already hearing the EMTs shouting to the nurses, begging them to work faster.

I burst into the ER and froze. Chaos had erupted. Nurses ran around, tripping over each other. There was blood everywhere. And at the center of the carnage, the patient. There was so much blood, it was difficult to tell right away what was wrong.

"What do we have?" I asked the nearest nurse. It happened to be Piper.

"Car accident. Two fatalities. This one made it through, but she's barely holding on. Broken ribs, a punctured lung, two serious breaks on her leg. The EMTs stabilized her leg, but we need to focus on—"

"Get her to operating room one!" I shouted, interrupting Piper. Yes, we needed to focus on the lungs, I *knew* that. If we didn't stabilize her, we were going to lose her. A punctured lung wasn't a joke.

The patient's face was covered in blood. It looked like she had taken a hit to the head, too.

"I'm going to need every hand on board," I barked.

Two more doctors were in the operating room with me, having scrubbed in as fast as I had. There were a handful of nurses, too. We needed as many hands as we could get. We needed to stop the bleeding, stop her lung from collapsing, and stabilize her heartbeat that was through the roof, erratic, arrhythmic.

"I need more hands here," I barked as I inserted the tube into her chest, letting the excess air out.

I glanced up, noticing the nurses working on the broken leg. Bone pierced the skin, ivory and glistening in the bright lights.

It was going to take a while to patch her up, but we had to save her life to be able to do that.

"Needle," I demanded.

Piper was next to me, grabbing the packet of needles and fumbling to get it open. They fell to the floor, the needles sprinkling onto the tiles.

"Oh, God," she muttered. "I'm so sorry!"

"They're no use to me now," I shouted. "If this patient dies, that's on you, Nurse Edwards."

She blinked up at me, eyes wide, cheeks pale.

"I need another packet, now!"

Another nurse offered me a needle, and I grabbed it, doing what I had to do to save the patient's life.

It took three grueling hours for us to pull the patient through. Her heart had stopped beating twice. We had to use defibrillation both times.

But we had managed to save her, and by the time she was stable enough for me to step back, I was exhausted.

Just as I gave my final orders to the remaining staff, Piper came up to me.

"She's pregnant," she said in a hoarse voice.

I blinked at her. "What are you talking about?"

"I think she's in early pregnancy," she repeated.

I looked at the patient, who showed no visible signs of pregnancy. "There is no way for you to know that."

"Just test her," she said.

"Fine," I said, annoyed.

I ordered the test to be run. Finally, I stepped out of the operating room, pulling the latex gloves from my hands, wiping my brow with my wrist. After the patient had come in, the ER had settled down again, and I was relieved to know that the only other patient waiting was a boy who needed stitches.

Another doctor could take care of that. I beeped someone who would be able to help.

I left the ER and walked to the staff room where I sank onto one of the couches.

God, it had been so close. We had nearly lost her. It had been a madhouse in there, and it was a miracle she was alive at all. Later, we would find out what had happened. We would know what she had been through. It was going to be a long road to recovery for her, not to mention the emotional trauma when she found out that the other two passengers in the car with her had been killed.

I closed my eyes, trying to get rid of the tension.

Piper flashed before my eyes, her face pale, her expression shocked.

God, I had shouted at her. I had told her that the patient's death would be on her hands.

It had probably hurt her.

I hated the thought of being the one to hurt her feelings. I didn't want her to think of me that way.

But the moment that thought crossed my mind, I scowled.

So what if it hurt her? So what if she thought I was the bad guy?

We were working with people's *lives* here. One misstep and we could lose them. Especially in situations like that, especially in the ER. If Piper was so soft that she couldn't handle how I had treated her, she didn't belong in the medical world.

Besides, she was a medical professional just like everyone else. It shouldn't have mattered how she felt after I had shouted at her. I treated all the nurses the same. None of the others had had a breakdown or quit their jobs because of how I treated them. Why should things be any different with Piper?

There was no reason to coddle her.

I scrubbed my face with my hands and shook my head, trying to get rid of the feeling of remorse. I would have shouted at any nurse who did what she had done. Sure, people made mistakes—human beings always did. But we couldn't afford to be weak. When things went wrong, we picked ourselves up and kept moving. We did what needed to be done.

It wasn't any different with Piper. She was one of my staff members. She'd have to suck it up like the rest of them.

In the ER, there was no space for emotion. The moment feelings snuck in, lives were lost. It was a quick-thinking, fast-acting game where we couldn't afford to make mistakes. We couldn't afford to stop and think. We had to act in the moment, rely on reflex and instinct. Nothing else mattered. Everything else had to take a backseat to what was happening right there, right then.

It took me a while to pull myself back together. I couldn't afford to fall apart, either, I reminded myself. I held myself to the same standard I held my nurses. I had to stay strong, push away any emotion. That was how it worked here.

I just had to keep reminding myself of that.

My stomach rumbled, and I realized I hadn't finished

my food in the cafeteria during lunch. I walked back to the cafeteria, hoping Nate would be around.

But the cafeteria was empty save for a couple of seats taken by nurses who had been in the ER with me.

I noticed Piper at one of the tables, hunched over, clutching a cup of coffee as if it would save her from going under.

My heart went out to her. For a moment, I wanted to go to her, to ask her if she was okay.

Before I could, Adriana appeared at her table and sat down, taking her hand.

It was enough to snap me out of my moment of weakness.

What was I doing? The nurses were there for each other. That was what friends were for. It wasn't my job to make sure Piper was okay. It wasn't my job to walk on eggshells around her, considering her unprofessional emotions.

I turned and left the cafeteria, walking to my office. I had paperwork that needed to be done. I had to find out what had happened to the patient, see if there were any other problems after more tests had been done by the doctors and nurses in the ICU. The patient had a long road ahead of her, and I wanted to make sure she was okay, that she would get through this alive.

She's pregnant. Her words echoed in my mind, and I shook my head. Where the hell had that come from? I couldn't tell her she was wrong, not medically. I didn't have proof. But neither did she.

In any case, we'd know soon enough, and we'd keep her and the baby safe, if there was one. But I was betting Piper had been shooting off her mouth.

Hadn't she told me about some airy-fairy meditation she

did? Was I supposed to believe she was on a higher plane where her female intuition could diagnose patients?

I laughed at the idea.

I had to refocus on my work. Not on the new nurse who seemed to make my mind spin out of control. Not on the woman who changed everything every time she walked into the room.

Soon, the novelty was going to wear off, and Piper would just be another nurse. I could get back to thinking about what was important.

I couldn't wait for that day to come.

Someone knocked on my door, and Nate pushed it open.

"So, it turns out you were right. It was the eye of the hurricane."

I sighed. "It's not easy always being right," I said, only half joking.

"And modest as hell," Nate said with a chuckle. "You're going to cope with this?"

"Of course," I said. "Don't I always?"

Nathan pulled up his shoulders. "I just lost one of my cancer patients. He fought for years. But it's over now." He sighed. "I could use a drink. How about you?"

"Yeah, sure," I said, standing.

We left my office, walking down the corridor to the main entrance of the hospital.

But suddenly, a flurry of movement caught my eye. I had a feeling I wouldn't be getting that drink, after all.

EIGHT

PIPER

The aftermath of the ER hit me hard. I usually managed to keep my head, but sometimes, there was too much blood, too much pain, and we got too close to death.

This time, the patient—a Kayla Sampson—had had death dig its claws into her so aggressively, we'd had to yank her back twice. It had left me shaken.

We'd done it, though. We'd pulled her through. Now, she was fighting to survive in an ICU with other nurses and doctors watching her.

I just couldn't seem to bounce back from what I'd seen. This time, it had been worse than usual. I'd seen a few bad cases come in through the ER doors during my years as a nurse. When you dealt with blood every day, you didn't feel faint at the sight of it anymore. But this time, I'd felt shaky, terrified of what might come.

Scared of losing her altogether.

I'd only lost a few so far. I hadn't wanted to add her to the list.

"Hey, are you okay?" Adriana asked when I was curled around a coffee cup in the cafeteria.

I nodded. "I'm fine."

"You don't look fine."

She sat down and took my hand. I didn't pull away. Instead, I curled my fingers around hers and squeezed, holding onto her, hoping she could pull me up so that I breached the surface again.

I felt like I was drowning.

"I should be able to deal with this stuff better," I said.

"It was a tough one," Adriana said.

And she was right. But she hadn't been right there in the operating room. She hadn't seen the way the patient had slipped away from us as if we hadn't been doing everything to hold her together.

If we hadn't been able to bring Kayla back... I shuddered, not wanting to picture the alternative.

"It's okay *not* to be okay, you know," Adriana said. "We don't see the usual things here. We deal with death and pain and blood and gore all the time. You just need to breathe through it. And get something stronger in your system than that cup of coffee you're nursing."

I smiled at Adriana. I was still in my first month at my new job, but already it felt like we were getting closer. She was here for me, and she understood what it was like.

Chris had never known exactly what I went through. When I'd been rattled because a patient had died when I'd been on rotation, he hadn't understood how it had felt like a part of me had been ripped away, too.

And as much as my family had tried to understand, they'd never been able to reach me through the haze that seemed to separate those who knew what it was like first-hand and those who only heard about it.

It was good to be friends with someone who knew what it was like. I'd never been so close to any of the nurses I'd worked with back home.

"I might take your advice about something stronger and go to bed with a bottle of vodka tonight," I said.

Adriana squeezed my hand. "You did great. You did what you could. You gave it your all, and that's all we can do."

I nodded, and she stood to get back to work. I had to do the same. I had to pull myself together and keep moving forward.

This wasn't the first time I'd fallen apart after an intense situation in the ER. But I felt weak every time I did. I had chosen this life. I had studied to become a nurse, and I had volunteered for the ER when we'd had that choice.

Feeling emotional was just going to drag me down and distract me from any future patients I needed to save.

I continued with the rest of my rounds, focusing on the lives we had saved, the people who were still alive and well. Those who would get to go home today, tomorrow, or maybe in a day or two.

That was what I kept telling myself while I visited one patient after the other and continued my chores. These were the people whose lives we had saved, people I had to look after. It was my job as a nurse to be positive on their behalf, to know that they would pull through, even though they didn't know it themselves. If I didn't trust that they would make it, how could they believe in themselves?

It was that kind of positivity that got me through the rest of the day. I checked on my patients, and none of them knew that inside, I was struggling with the pain of what I had seen.

I kept an eye on the clock, waiting for the moment

where I could knock off and go home. I needed to be in my own space to be able to fall apart completely.

I went to the locker room and got dressed in jeans and a T-shirt, getting out of my scrubs, trying to leave the hospital behind. But when I walked out of the staff locker room, an unexpected wave of emotion washed over me, and my eyes stung with tears.

I tried to swallow down the lump that rose in my throat, but I had run out of positive energy. Tears rolled over my cheeks, and I swallowed back a sob that racked my chest.

Oh, God. I couldn't let anyone see me like this—not the other nurses and not the patients. I was supposed to be on top of it, keeping it together. This was my job, after all. I had to keep a straight face, a smile, plastered on at all times.

I backed away from the busy front lobby, struggling to keep back the sobs, and headed toward a patient room I knew was empty. I closed the door behind me and covered my face with my hands, letting myself break down.

I shouldn't have been that emotional. It wasn't right. Things like this were bound to happen all the time.

But it wasn't just the pain, the trauma, that had reduced me to tears.

It was the fact that Ethan had treated me like shit.

I couldn't stand working for a man who would treat me as Ethan had. He'd shouted at me for making a mistake in a situation where everything had been tense and difficult.

I had known that it was a dumb mistake to drop those needles, but surely, he could have understood the pressure we were all under. And then he hadn't believed me about Kayla being pregnant.

I didn't know how I'd known. But I knew for a fact that she was. We acted on instinct all the time. And mine was strong.

Ethan had to trust me. But he didn't.

He'd made it look like I was crazy for even suggesting something like that. But it wasn't impossible, and if she was pregnant, it might have put her in a whole new kind of danger.

For some reason, my mind jumped back to Chris. This situation wasn't the same. I had dated Chris, and he had expected me to support both of us. Ethan was different. He was my boss, albeit difficult and impossible to work with.

But I had just removed myself from an unhealthy relationship. I wasn't going to be treated badly again.

Not even by a coworker.

At some point, I had to draw a line.

I tried to swallow my tears. I rubbed my face with my hands, getting rid of the tears that stained my cheeks. I was going to walk out of there and no one would know that I'd taken a moment to lose it.

"You go on ahead," I heard a male voice outside the door. "I'll catch up with you."

I swallowed my sobs and tried to keep perfectly still, waiting until the person on the other side of the door moved on.

But the door opened, and I held my breath.

"Piper," the deep, smooth voice said, and I realized it was Ethan. He had found me in my hiding spot. He stepped inside, closing the door behind him.

"Ethan."

"That's Dr. Cole to you."

God, he was such an asshole. After what we had been through together, surely, I could call him Ethan. I wasn't talking about us saving lives together, either.

"What are you doing here?" I asked.

"I saw you come in here."

He didn't say anything else. For a moment, we were caught in a limbo of sorts, neither of us knowing what to say.

"And?" I asked. "The room isn't occupied. I just needed a moment."

"Yeah, I noticed."

His voice was clipped. If he had noticed that I needed some time alone, why had he followed me here?

"Okay," I said.

For a moment, I saw in him the man I had met at the bar, charming and handsome. But the familiarity only flickered across his features for a moment before his seriousness returned.

"You're upset," he said.

"We all are," I defended. "It was tough in there."

"This career is tough," Ethan said. "You can't fall apart when something goes wrong. When you work in this career, you need to leave your emotions at the door and act like a professional."

I blinked at him. "It's not like I'm falling apart in the operating room."

"No, but you came close."

I was getting angry, the anger replacing my shock.

But I was also flustered as I felt his gaze burning my skin. If only he weren't so damned good-looking. It would be easier to talk to him if he weren't so *hot*.

"Fumbling in the operating room isn't the same as coming undone at the seams."

"To me, there is no difference. You need to be on top of your game, Piper."

He didn't refer to me as Nurse Edwards, I realized. But he had a problem with me calling him by his first name?

But I was quickly getting too angry to worry about that.

"Look, I wasn't unprofessional. I didn't let my emotions

get in the way." I clenched my hands into fists. "The fact that I'm struggling now shouldn't be a problem. It's away from everyone, and technically, it's on my own time."

"Are you still on the premises?" Ethan asked.

I gaped at him. Was he seriously going to expect me to be perfect at all times while I was at the hospital? Even the great Ethan Cole couldn't be so heartless that nothing affected him.

"Look, I know you have a good name," I snapped. "I've heard about you as far as Roanoke. But don't think it means that you can treat people the way you do. I have feelings, too."

"And you act on them!" Ethan cried out.

"Not when it matters."

Ethan took a step closer to me. "This is exactly when it matters."

I was aware of how close he was to me, how intense his eyes were, his chest rising and falling with his breath. His masculine scent—leather and pine—filled my senses, disorienting me.

I flashed on the last time he was this close, breathing this hard.

"Really?" I asked, but my voice had turned breathy. "Is this when it matters?"

Ethan's eyes slid to my lips. I didn't know if he'd meant to look or if it happened involuntarily, but suddenly, he grabbed me and kissed me. His hands bracketed my face, and his tongue slid into my mouth.

I surrendered to the intoxicating sensation, the taste and the feel of him. The anger inside me melted into something hotter, something more urgent.

I wrapped my arms around his neck, and he pulled me closer. His body was taut, his cock hard where it ground against my stomach, and the room around us was suddenly hot, my clothes itching on my skin. I wanted to get rid of them.

God, I wanted him. I wanted him to touch me, to strip me naked. I wanted him to do what he had done the last time we were together. I wanted him to fuck me.

I wanted him to take away all the pain and replace it with something warm and full.

Ethan seemed to be on the same track. He spun me around and walked me toward the hospital bed in the empty room.

We were all alone, and anything could happen.

And I knew exactly what I *wanted* to happen.

NINE

ETHAN

She was soft underneath my hands, her skin hot through her clothes. She had dressed out of her scrubs, and for some reason, that just made me want to strip her down and get her naked even more.

Maybe it wouldn't have mattered what she wore, as long as she wasn't wearing it anymore.

My cock throbbed, yearning to be inside her again.

In my mind, I did the calculations. The room was unassigned to a patient, which meant no one was going to enter it again until the cleaning staff arrived the next day. We wouldn't be disturbed. No one would know what we were doing in here, and as long as we kept quiet, we were both going to get what we wanted.

What we *needed.*

My hands slid underneath Piper's thin shirt. I felt her breasts through her lace bra, her nipples erect in my palms. I eased her back onto the bed and climbed onto her. Her breath came in rapid gasps. She opened her legs to let me grind myself against her.

I slid my hand down her flat little stomach and into her jeans. My fingers pushed into her slit. She was already wet.

Dripping wet.

She moaned when I ran my fingers over her clit. God, I couldn't get *enough* of her.

Suddenly, she pulled back.

"Stop," she whispered, and I froze.

"What's wrong?"

"We can't do this."

She wrapped her fingers around my wrist and pulled my hand out of her pants. Her eyes were drowning deep when she looked at me, but her lips were pursed into a thin line.

Suddenly, I blinked.

What was I doing? How could I have let it go this far?

I cleared my throat and climbed off the bed, taking a step back. My cock was straining against my pants, my heart hammering against my ribs, but logical thought was starting to return.

"Right," I said curtly. I took a few breaths, looking at the floor and willing my erection to die down as I heard her get off the bed. Finally, I turned around, and left the room.

I wasn't running away, I told myself. I was *walking* away, doing the right thing.

How the hell could I have let this happen? How could I have let lust take over like that?

Shit, I could have gotten fired for my behavior.

It wasn't against hospital policy to date within the hospital, but having sex in one of the hospital rooms? It was completely inappropriate.

I shouldn't have lost control like that.

I tugged at my collar, trying to catch my breath as I walked through the hospital, blindly turning from one hallway to the next. I was glad Nate hadn't waited for me. Luckily, I had told him to go on ahead, that I would meet him at The Tavern.

Dammit, I was such a fool! To let my body take over like a damned teenager? I hadn't done something like that since... well, ever.

Piper was some kind of kryptonite. When I was around her, I didn't think clearly.

There was just something about her.

She was kind. She was caring. When she worked with patients, she invested herself. She got attached, but not in a bad way. She cared about their lives, about who they were as people, and what we could do for them.

She gave a piece of her heart.

It was incredibly sexy.

I thought about how she had reacted in the operating room.

She's pregnant.

There had been no way in hell she could have known.

I turned down the next hallway and headed toward the lab.

My mind was reeling. I needed to know for sure if Piper had been right.

Would it help me get over her, forget about her? God, I didn't know if anything would help me stop thinking about her. But I had to know if she'd been right.

If she had, she had an incredible premonition about things, and she was an even better nurse than anyone knew.

"What do you have for me?" I asked Julie, the lab tech. "Give me the good news."

Julie smiled at me and turned to a file. "You can't just come in here making demands, Ethan."

I grinned at her. "No? I have it on good authority that it's exactly what I'm allowed to do."

"And to think, you could have come in here to ask me out for a drink instead."

I shook my head with a chuckle. Julie was flirting with me again.

But she wasn't my type. And even if she were, she'd be a far second when it came to Piper.

"Here you go," she said, giving me a stack of papers and smiling at me.

I took them from her and started paging through. There were a couple of different tests, but I ignored the results. I wanted to know if Piper had been right.

When I found Kayla Sampson's bloodwork, my eyes moved to the bottom of the page. I stilled, my blood running cold.

Pregnant. She was pregnant.

"Did you see this?" I asked, pointing to the page.

"Yeah, the HCG was incredibly low, so low I had to run the bloods twice to be sure. But it's there, all right. I doubt the patient even knows herself. Home pregnancy tests wouldn't have picked up on it. It's very, very early."

"That might be what will save the baby. Did you let Dr. Carter know?" I asked.

Julie nodded. "Of course. It's not the kind of thing you forget to mention in a case like this."

I nodded. It was serious if Ms. Sampson was pregnant. It affected how she would be treated, what medications they could give her, and what would happen if she needed to be operated on.

How the hell could Piper have known that?

God, I needed to apologize to her. I needed to talk to

her, to tell her that after everything I had said to her, I had been wrong.

It wasn't going to be easy, but I had to do it. And it would be wrong of me to act like I had been right to treat her the way I had.

At some point, a man had to stick his pride in his pocket.

Piper had already left the hospital for the evening, but I knew where she lived.

I wouldn't have forgotten where she lived or anything else about that night. No matter how drunk we'd been.

Going to her house was probably a mistake. After what had happened between us in the hospital room, it was inappropriate for me to visit her at all. But to talk to her at the hospital about what had happened between us would be worse. And I did need to speak to her.

After what had happened between us—when we had met at the bar and now that we'd gone at each other in the hospital room—we needed to figure out where we stood and what we were going to do.

The drive to her home was a short one, much shorter than I was comfortable with. I would have liked more time to figure out what I was going to say to her, give her a proper reason for why I knocked on her door.

I pulled up, and my headlights lit up her house, falling on the living room windows.

The door opened a moment later. Dammit, she knew someone was there.

I climbed out of the car as she stepped onto the porch.

"What are you doing here?" she asked, her arms folded over her chest.

"I need to talk to you."

"I have nothing to say to you."

I sighed, walking closer to her. "I know, and I don't blame you. But... just hear me out. You don't have to say anything. Just listen."

She narrowed her eyes at me, and I could see her trying to decide if she was going to tell me to piss off. I would leave if that was what she wanted.

But I hoped that she wasn't going to make me leave.

"Fine," she finally said and turned back into the house. She didn't invite me in, but the fact that she didn't close the door in my face was enough to make me follow her inside.

TEN

PIPER

I had no idea what Ethan was doing here. I wasn't interested in talking to him. Every interaction with him at the hospital had been either riddled with so much lust I choked on it or so cold I needed a sweater.

The latter had made me resent him. I didn't want to talk to him. I didn't want to hear what he had to say.

But he'd asked so damn nicely. And since that was rare for him, I wasn't able to say no.

My mind jumped to Chris and how many times I'd taken him back, how many times I'd forgiven him for being wrong when I'd known I shouldn't have.

But this wasn't the same, was it? Ethan was my boss.

And a part of me wanted to know what he had to say.

Okay, and another part of me was still swooning from our little make-out session at the hospital today. His touch on my skin, his breath on my neck...

But that wasn't going to happen again.

And if he was rude, I was going to kick him out right away. This wasn't the hospital where he was above me in the pecking order. This was my home. I was the queen of my castle.

And no one, not even some Adonis with a lab coat, was going to disturb my peace.

In the living room, I turned to him, my arms still folded over my chest, and I glared at him. Ethan closed the door behind him as if I'd invited him to stay for a real visit. I didn't tell him to open the door again.

He could do that on his way out. However soon that would be.

I tried to look sullen, angry. But I was unsure now that he was in my house. He was larger than life, his attitude spilling into the corners of the room. I saw Charlie bolt into the spare bedroom before Ethan could even see him.

"And?" I asked, wishing he'd say something.

"I was hoping we could talk," Ethan said.

"You said you had something to say."

He nodded. "Can I sit down?"

I didn't want him to say that long but saying no would be ridiculous.

"Sure."

Ethan sat down. From the spare bedroom, I heard a faint rustling noise. Charlie was up to no good in there, but I ignored it.

"Look, about what happened at the hospital earlier..."

"It won't happen again," I said quickly. "You made it very clear. Even though you were the one to instigate it."

He blinked at me. "Oh, I didn't mean... I was talking about in the operating room. I'm sorry I shouted at you."

I frowned at him. "You're apologizing?"

He nodded.

"Why?"

He hesitated just a moment. "Well, you were right."

I gaped at him. "I don't think I understand."

He chuckled. "I don't say those words often, but you were correct. Kayla Sampson is pregnant. I got the test results from the lab just before I came here. I should have listened to you. But it just seemed so unlikely."

"I told you," I said, a bit more confident than I felt. I had instincts, and I always followed them. But honestly, my gut wasn't *always* right. Sometimes, I was wrong.

Something crashed to the floor in the spare bedroom. Ethan jumped up and whirled around.

"What was that?" he asked, immediately on guard and ready to face down whatever intruder was in the house.

Instead, a blur of spotted fur came at him.

Charlie shot out of the room like a bullet, running through Ethan's legs. Ethan yelped and backed up, nearly tripping over my coffee table to get away from the hellion cat. Charlie ricocheted off the couch and then jumped into my arms and started to purr.

I burst out laughing.

"Is that a demon or a cat?" Ethan asked.

"Meet Charlie," I said, still laughing. "You should see your expression. You stare death in the face on the daily, but you're afraid of a cat?"

"I just got a scare," Ethan said, looking sheepish. "I didn't know what it was. This guy's fierce."

"Charlie looks for trouble when he knows I'm busy with something else."

Ethan looked at Charlie in my arms, his eyes moving over the cat's spots. "Looks like a leopard."

"He's a Bengal," I cooed, holding Charlie up to show him off.

"You didn't strike me as a cat person," Ethan said.

I giggled. "What kind of person did you think I was?"

Ethan pulled up his shoulders and slowly came closer, reaching his hand out so Charlie could sniff his fingers. He wasn't just rushing forward and grabbing Charlie, and I appreciated that he was so sweet about it.

"I don't know," he finally said. "I guess I don't really know you at all."

I smiled. The tension between us had broken completely. Now that Ethan was here, away from the pressures and demands of the hospital, he was the guy from the bar again. Easygoing, charming, fun.

Not to mention the way he'd sprung to his feet as if to defend me from an intruder had been a little sexy.

To my total surprise, I suddenly wanted to spend more time with him—with *this* Ethan.

It was a chance I was taking, but I didn't want him to leave any time soon.

"I was just about to make something to eat," I said, jabbing a thumb in the direction of the kitchen where pasta was already simmering on the stove. "Do you want to stay for supper?"

Ethan hesitated.

"If you can't, I get it," I added quickly.

"No, I want to," he said. "I just... This is looking for trouble."

"I know," I said softly.

He looked at Charlie, scratching him behind the ears.

"He doesn't usually like strangers," I said.

"He's a cutie."

I nodded. "Yeah. He's my baby."

Ethan looked up at me with dark eyes and smiled. "I'd love to stay for supper."

"Are you sure?"

"Yeah. I mean... I love cats. And you have this little guy."

"Right," I giggled and set Charlie down. "So glad you could make a friend."

Ethan chuckled and walked to the kitchen with me.

"What can I help with?" he asked. "What's going with the pasta?"

"I was going to throw a can of tomato sauce and a pack of bacon into it," I said.

Ethan frowned at me. "What?"

I felt silly. "I'm not much of a cook." I had asked him to stay because I didn't want him to leave. I hadn't thought about my skills in the kitchen—or lack thereof.

"I guess bacon and tomato with pasta can be great. But... a salad with it, maybe? If you have ingredients, I'll chop one up for us." It was his turn to look like he felt silly. "You know, if you don't think it's rude of me to renovate your menu for the evening."

I smiled and shook my head. "I don't mind."

Ethan pointed at the fridge, a question on his face, and when I nodded, he walked to it and started taking out salad ingredients.

I could hardly believe Ethan was back in my house, helping me make dinner. And I was enjoying it.

I took out a chopping board for him, and he settled in at the breakfast counter, chopping tomatoes and cucumber with the precision of a surgeon. I glanced at him while I fried the bacon. He was a perfectionist. I imagined everything in his life was just so. I was far from a slob, but I wasn't nearly as set on having everything perfectly arranged or set in its place, or my salad cut into even cubes.

"What?" he asked when he looked up as I was staring at him.

"Nothing." I tried to swallow a smile. "Are you in the operating room often?"

"Are you mocking me?" he asked, a smile playing around his mouth, too.

I shook my head. "No, no. I'm just watching you dissect the tomato as if you're going to stitch it up again and give it a new life once you're done with it."

Ethan chuckled. "Everything you do should be with excellence in mind."

I giggled. "Even one-night stands?"

"Especially one-night stands," he said with a dark laugh.

I blushed. I'd meant to call him out. Instead, he was putting me on the spot. He'd been damn *excellent* that night, and I couldn't deny it.

A shiver ran through my core as I recalled his body against mine, his fingers on my skin... I cleared my throat and brought my mind back to the present.

I dumped the sauce and bacon into the pasta, mixed it through, and walked to the breakfast counter with two plates, knives, and forks. The salad had come out beautifully. The meal was suddenly something great, a lot more than I would have bothered making. We sat together and started eating.

"This is surprisingly good," Ethan said.

I laughed. "Surprisingly?"

"I didn't think it would work, but it does."

I took a bite, sucking a strand of spaghetti between my lips.

"Tell me about yourself," I said.

Ethan groaned. "That's a cliché line."

"I just see this one side of you at work, and now I'm seeing a totally different version of you. It's a mystery. What else am I supposed to ask?" I asked with a laugh.

"Something more specific. Otherwise, I might as well give you my resume."

I grinned at him. "You want me to ask you specific things? That seems very dangerous for someone so intent on keeping me at arm's length."

He blinked at me. "Who says that's what I'm trying to do? I stayed for supper."

"I'm a woman, Ethan, not a lump of clay. I can figure shit out for myself, you know. You have a *Keep Out* sign nailed to your forehead where the world can see it."

He frowned at me, his expression shifting a little, and I worried I'd ruined the evening.

"What made you become a doctor?" I asked, trying to shift the topic to something a little lighter than whatever went on in his mind.

It worked. His face brightened again.

"I wanted to help people."

"Since you were a kid?"

He shook his head. "No, that only came later. After my parents passed away."

I stilled. "I'm sorry."

"Thank you. I just realized I needed to do something with my life. When I tried to figure out what it was, it felt simple enough. Everyone out there needs help in one way or another. At least, this way, I get to help some of them."

"But not all of them," I said softly.

"You can't save everyone."

We sat in silence for a moment, his words hanging in the air between us. He was right. For some reason, it made me think of Chris. I'd done everything for him, thinking I could get him to be a better man. But I couldn't save him because he hadn't wanted to be saved.

You can't save everyone.

"What about you?" Ethan asked. "Why a nurse?"

"Because doctors are above the average human. Someone has to pick up the pieces and level with them," I said with a cheeky smile.

For a moment, Ethan looked shocked, but then he laughed and shook his head.

"You're something else, Piper."

I smiled up at him. He gazed at me intensely.

Suddenly, he took my chin between his thumb and forefinger and carefully turned my head to him, his lips pressing against mine.

It was a surprise, but I melted against him as our mouths moved together. Finally, we pulled apart just a bit to look at each other.

"What was that?" I asked in a breathy voice.

"I can't help myself when I'm with you," he said. His voice was deep, hoarse, and it tugged at my insides.

I kissed him, leaning in for a second round. Suddenly, my appetite for dinner was gone, but my hunger for him had become ravenous.

I wanted him to touch me. I wanted him to undress me.

"Where's your room?" he asked in a gruff voice as if he knew what I was thinking.

I smiled. "My room?"

"The couch isn't going to cut it tonight," he said, a smile spreading over his face.

I nodded and stood. He took my hand, intertwining our fingers, and I led him through the house to the bedroom.

Ethan pulled me against him when we were in my room and kissed me again. His arms were wrapped around my body, and he ground himself against me. His cock was rock hard in his jeans.

The heat in my body pooled between my legs, making me wet. I moaned.

"When you do that, you just make me want you more," he growled.

"When I do what?"

He ground himself against me again, and I moaned another time.

"That," he whispered.

The atmosphere in the room was thick. My breathing was shallow. Heat stretched between us, drawing us closer.

I was melting into my panties. The length of his cock pushed up against my crotch, all the way up my lower stomach. I needed his hands on my skin. I ached for him in a way I'd never ached for anyone.

"I want you to fuck me, Ethan," I whispered.

He groaned and rolled his hips, pushing himself against me. He kissed me while he did, softly at first, pushing his tongue into my mouth. I loved the way he explored my mouth, probing, asking for more. His hands slid into my hair, closing into a fist, and he tugged back lightly, tilting my head up.

He worked his way down my neck, planting a trail of fire as far as he went. I squirmed, trembling with need for him. My body begged for release. I wanted him to touch me, to push his fingers into the slick wetness between my legs.

I ran my hands down Ethan's body, resting them on his hips. He pushed his hips forward, and I slid my hands onto his firm ass, squeezing.

God, he was fucking *delicious.*

When we'd been together before, we'd both been a little drunk. Now, I was very, very sober. And nothing about him was a disappointment. It was just as good as before.

"You have no idea how much I want you," Ethan

murmured, moving back to my mouth, his lips only fractions away from mine. "I want to pin you down and taste every inch of you."

I gasped.

"And when I'm done tasting, I want more. I want to fuck you, slowly at first, and then hard and fast until your neighbors know my name."

His words were only turning me on more and more.

"I want to bury my cock deep inside of you. I want to feel every inch of your body."

I moaned, trailing my fingers up his muscular back, and he rolled his hips another time.

I started pushing up Ethan's shirt, rolling it over his perfect body. When did he find time to lift weights when he worked as hard as he did?

He helped me get rid of his shirt. I ran my hands over his skin, the thick muscles rippling beneath it, and he was hot to the touch.

"Tell me, Piper," Ethan said in a whisper. "Tell me what you want."

I moaned. "I want you."

"You want me to what?"

He lifted my shirt over my chest, and he thumbed the lining of my bra cups. I shivered, my skin burning in anticipation of his touch, but he didn't touch me yet—not really. It made me ache for him, only increased my need for him.

"Please," I whispered. His lips brushed against mine, but when I leaned in to kiss him, he pulled away a little, teasing.

"What, Piper?" he asked.

"Fuck me," I said hoarsely.

He let out a throaty growl and kissed me, hard, before he pulled my shirt over my head. He started kissing me down my neck again, hands snaking around my body to unclasp my bra. It joined my shirt, and his, on the floor.

Ethan took my hand and led me to the bed, nudging me so that I lay down on it. I lay on my back, topless, and Ethan looked at me with eyes that were riddled with hunger and desire for me.

He stared at me with fierce intensity as I lay spread out before him. I felt like a delicacy he was about to devour.

I fucking *loved* it.

He dipped his head and kissed me before he moved to my breasts.

He sucked one nipple into his mouth, and I moaned as he started swirling his tongue around it, the other hand skillfully kneading my other breast. It sent a direct message to my pussy. I arched my back, tipped back my head, and moaned as I closed my eyes and got lost in the sensation.

He was worshipping my body as if he'd never been with a woman before. As if he considered me the most beautiful and desirable woman in the world.

He slid his hand down my abdomen and toward my jeans. He undid my pants and worked them down my body. I helped, wriggling free of them, kicking them to the side.

He gazed at me for a moment, taking my whole body in. When I couldn't wait any longer, I guided Ethan's hand between my legs where I needed him to be. When his fingers pushed into my slit, he groaned.

"Fuck," he bit out. "You're so wet."

"That's how much I want you," I said.

Ethan plunged his fingers into me and started pumping, and I gasped and moaned, all thoughts leaving my mind.

Ethan shifted, and suddenly he was between my legs, parting my thighs with his hands. He rolled his thumb over my sensitive folds. I moaned as he played with my clit, pushing his fingers slowly in and out of me at the same time. I shivered and cried out as he brought me closer to an orgasm.

"I want to taste you," Ethan said. "And then I want to be inside of you so that I can feel you come."

He pushed his fingers in and out of me a few more times, and suddenly, he dipped his head between my thighs and closed his mouth over my pussy. I moaned and cried out when he ran his tongue over my clit. He flicked his tongue over me a few times, his fingers still deep inside of me, and it felt like something incredible was going to erupt inside of me. He licked and sucked my folds, his fingers filling me, and I moaned and cried out. Something delicious grew inside of me.

I moved my hands to my breasts, tweaking my nipples, writhing on the bed as the heat at my core grew and grew, threatening to swallow me.

"Come for me, babe," Ethan said softly, and as if on command, I came undone. The orgasm ripped through me, and I cried out, curling on the bed, bucking my hips against his mouth as Ethan balanced me between his mouth and his fingers deep inside of me. I rode out the wave of pleasure that overcame me.

When I came down from my sexual high, Ethan crawled over me and kissed me. I could taste myself on his lips. His hands roamed my body, and I trembled in the aftermath of the orgasm that had just rocked me to my core.

"I'll be right back," Ethan said and climbed off the bed. He unzipped his jeans, stepped out of them, and I watched as he ripped open a condom foil. He rolled it over his erection without ceremony and came back to the bed, hard, bobbing with every step he took.

When he crawled over me again, my thighs fell open for

him, and he pushed his cock up against my entrance. My stomach tightened, and I held my breath in anticipation for what was to follow.

Ethan slid into me, and I felt him stretch my body, pushing his way into me. Ethan buried himself to the hilt, and I shivered around him.

"Fuck." His face was riddled with lust, his eyes dark and deep. "You feel incredible."

I kissed him, wrapping my arms around his neck.

"I'm going to fuck you nice and slow," he said as he started moving inside of me.

I had thought the sex was good after we'd been drinking. This was a whole new level. I moaned when he withdrew and then slowly pushed back into me.

"I'm going to take my time and learn every inch of your body until you can't take it anymore and you beg me to fuck you hard and fast."

I smiled. "You're going to make me beg?"

Ethan nodded and slid out of me again, staying there, his cock barely inside of me. I shivered, shifting my hips, moaning, but he didn't give me what I wanted.

"Give it to me," I whispered. He chuckled. "Please," I begged.

He kissed me and pushed into me again. But it was slow —torturously so.

Ethan started moving faster and faster, his cock sliding in and out of me, and I cried out in rhythm.

"I thought you were going to keep it slow," I gasped when he started fucking me faster and faster.

"I changed my mind. You're irresistible."

I giggled, but my laughter faded when he started fucking me even faster, creating a new sensation of pleasure that washed over me, pushing me toward a second orgasm.

His hips bucked against me. The sound of our sex filled the room as we gasped and moaned together.

The second orgasm came suddenly and took me by surprise. I cried out, curling my body around his.

I trembled and shivered on the bed, and Ethan slowed down, holding still while I tried to rebuild myself where I'd fallen apart.

He pulled out of me a moment later and rolled onto his back.

"Get on top of me," he said.

I did what he asked. I straddled his hips and sank onto his cock. When I did, we moaned in unison. He gripped my hips, and I started moving back and forth, sliding him in and out of me. It took me only a moment to adjust to his size from this angle, and then I picked up my pace.

Ethan's eyes were glued to my breasts as they bounced while I rode him, and his brows knit together in concentration.

"I can't last much longer with you on top of me," he bit out.

I smiled. "Then don't."

I rocked harder and faster, and Ethan's fingers dug into my skin as he pulled me toward him and pushed me back, helping me fuck him harder than I would have, helping me keep my rhythm.

He was getting closer, and I could feel him grow thick and hard inside of me. I moaned loudly.

"You're going to make me lose my load if you sound like that," Ethan said.

"I can't help it," I moaned, gasping, breathless, and a moment later, Ethan gripped my hips hard, jerked inside of me, and I sat down hard on him. I felt his cock pulsate as he came inside of me. He bit out curse words, his hands on my thighs. I felt an echo of my orgasm and gasped and moaned while he came inside of me.

Finally, when it died down, I collapsed on his chest.

Ethan was getting soft inside of me. I lifted my hips so he could slip out, and he reached between us and caught the condom. I rolled onto my side on the bed and he stood. He disappeared into the bathroom for just a moment before he came back and lay down next to me again.

He pulled me tightly against him, wrapping his arm around my shoulder. I sighed and pressed my cheek against his chest.

Everything was perfect.

It was hard to imagine this was the same man I worked with at the hospital who barked orders at me all day long.

But I wasn't going to think about that now. He was here with me, and he wasn't treating me badly at all. In fact, he'd treated me like a queen. Like a goddess. That was all that mattered.

What would happen tomorrow or the day after, or the day after that? I had no idea.

But that could wait until later.

ELEVEN

ETHAN

Waking up next to Piper was better than anything I could have imagined.

I hadn't woken up next to a woman in years. I'd had a girlfriend for a while in college, but we'd broken up soon after my parents' sudden death. Our relationship hadn't been strong enough to survive the aftermath, the grieving. Since then, one-night stands had been my thing.

My definition of a one-night stand did *not* include waking up next to a woman. Cuddling, sleeping next to each other, cooking breakfast together... Those were the mark of a relationship. I'd never been interested in complicating things with the women I slept with.

With Piper, everything was different, though.

For one, I enjoyed sleeping next to her. And holding onto her. Cuddling her.

I tried not to think too hard about what it all meant.

When I opened my eyes that morning, she lay on my chest as if we hadn't moved all night. Her hair was splayed over my shoulder, her long lashes brushing her cheeks, her breathing even.

I wanted to go to the bathroom, but I didn't want to wake her. So I lay in bed, studying the light on her strawberry blonde hair.

When she shifted and blinked sleepy eyes up at me, I smiled.

"You're still here," she said in a husky voice.

God, I could wake up to this perfect image every day.

I shook off the thoughts.

"I am," I said with a smile. "But I'm making you late, I'm sure."

Piper shook her head. "I have the day off. What time are you going in?"

"I've got an afternoon shift. Not until after lunch."

Piper nodded. "Stay for breakfast?"

"Only if I get to cook."

Piper giggled. "Fine, you can take over my kitchen. I'll pretend that I'm not offended."

For a moment, I worried that she *was* offended, but when she smiled up at me, her eyes twinkling with amusement, I realized she was joking.

She stretched, curling beneath the sheets. The outline of her incredible body was clear. I felt my cock harden again, ready for round two. But I wasn't going to give in. I was going to behave unless she instigated it. I hadn't stayed over just for the sake of having more sex.

Piper climbed out of bed and disappeared into the bathroom for a while. I stood, finding my boxers on the floor, and pulled them on. I found my T-shirt, too. I left my jeans where they were.

When Piper stepped out of the bathroom, still naked, I let my eyes roam her body.

"You're beautiful," I said.

She blushed lightly and gave me a smile. "Thanks, Ethan."

She walked to the closet, giving me a nice view of her heart-shaped ass, and pulled out a T-shirt that showed her midriff. She put on delicious lacy underwear that made me want to peel it off her again and wiggled her hips into a tight pair of cut-off shorts.

God, she was hot.

After she was dressed, she beckoned me to follow her to the kitchen.

Charlie sat on the floor, close to his bowl.

"Hello, handsome," Piper said, kneeling next to him to scratch between his ears before she filled his bowl with cat food. I watched her as she moved around the kitchen.

She was good with everyone and everything she talked to, it seemed. She was just as loving toward her cat as she was toward the patients in our ward.

Okay, maybe not quite the same, but it was close.

"You can go ahead and take out whatever you need," Piper said, looking up at me. "I have breed, eggs, milk, you go on ahead."

I nodded and opened the fridge, trying to decide what I was going to do. I settled on French toast and started preparing it while Piper made us coffee.

"So, what do you think of North Haven? Are you happy here?" I asked her while we moved around each other in the kitchen, easily fitting together as if we had done this a million times before.

"I'm getting there," Piper said. "It takes some getting used to. It's the first time I've moved away from home."

"You lived with your parents until now?"

She shook her head. "No, I recently went through a bad

breakup. But I never lived anywhere other than Roanoke, so it's an adjustment."

I took note of her dating history. A bad breakup. Recent. Well, that was enough reason for me not to get too involved. It should have been a relief, but I suddenly realized that I wanted to see her again. And not just to fuck, either.

I wanted to spend time with her the way we had last night, eating supper together. And the way we were now, making breakfast.

I didn't know how this had happened. I didn't date. But when I looked at Piper, I started to think that maybe I wanted to try.

There was something about her that was very different. It made me want to be around her, to get to know her better.

The moment I thought it, my stomach twisted, a knot settling in the pit of it.

What if it didn't work out? What if I ended up getting attached and lost her?

Wouldn't it be easier to not try at all? It was safer that way. But that would mean that I would have to break it off. I'd have to tell her that I wouldn't see her unless it was in a professional capacity.

And I knew I didn't want that. I wanted to see her after hours, I wanted to be casual with her. I wanted to flirt with her, court her. I wanted to be romantic with her.

What we had shared last night had been so much more than sex. I wouldn't admit that to her—not yet—but I wanted to try. I wanted to see how a relationship could go.

Even if it wouldn't last long. The only way I was going to find out if it worked for me was if I took that first step.

"Where are we going with this?" I asked, looking at Piper.

"What?" She asked, looking up at me. Her eyes were

bright, her lips slightly parted. I'd never seen a more beautiful vision in the morning.

"If this thing between us continues... Where are we going with it?"

She blinked at me. "I didn't know you wanted to go somewhere with this. I was pretty sure you were just looking for sex."

"Yeah, I didn't think I wanted to date, either. But maybe I want to give it a shot with you."

Piper had been looking at me over her shoulder while she had been preparing coffee, but she set everything down and turned to face me.

"Are you being serious?"

I nodded. "I know it's not usually done that people date in the workplace, but it's not against the rules. We'll just have to approach it right. Of course, only if you're interested."

Piper's face lit up and she giggled. "Interested? In you?"

I half expected a joke, something teasing, but she nodded. "I *am* interested," she finally said, as if in shock.

I laughed. "Why are you so surprised about it?"

"Because you can be a real ass," she said bluntly.

I walked to her, pulled her against me, and kissed her.

"That's only one side of me," I said, breaking the kiss. "You've seen the other side of me, too."

"And I happen to know you *have* a perfect ass, as well," she said with a smile.

I laughed again. I let go of her and turned back to the pan where the French toast was nearly burned.

"I think we should talk to HR," I said, flipping it over with a spatula. "We should let them know about our relationship. It's hospital policy."

"I guess we can do that," Piper said. "If you want to go public with it right away..."

I thought about it for a moment.

"Do you think we should wait?"

"I don't know. I think things are a little different for me as a nurse than they are for you. Won't it affect your career?"

I looked at her, frowning.

"Did you know about the promotion?"

Piper frowned and shook her head. "What promotion?"

I had a promotion coming up for medical director. It was a big deal. I had been hoping for this position for a long, long time. I hadn't mentioned it to anyone, though.

"I thought it strange that you mention it affecting my career," I said after explaining to Piper what was happening.

"I just heard that doctors don't usually mix with the nurses. I was thinking about your social reputation."

I chuckled. "If there is one thing I don't care about, it's what other people think about me."

Piper raised her eyebrows.

"What? Did you think I care?"

She pulled up her shoulders, smiled at me without answering, and started pouring coffee into the cups.

I shook my head, chuckling. She challenged me all the time, outright insulting me sometimes, joking at other times. And it never offended me. I could see why everyone liked her so much.

Hell, I liked her so much, too.

It wasn't forbidden for coworkers to date, but I was worried that the review board wouldn't be happy with our relationship. What if they thought I couldn't focus on my job because I was distracted by a new love?

"Maybe we should keep things professional at work for a while," I finally said. "When we know that this is what we want, we can come out with it, but we don't have to announce it right away."

Piper nodded, handing me the cup of coffee she had prepared. I put the last piece of French toast onto a plate and we carried our food and cups to the breakfast counter.

"I think that's a good idea," Piper agreed. "We can always spend time together outside of work."

I took a bite of my French toast and nodded. "You can stay at my place, for a change."

Piper smiled. "This *is* starting to look like a relationship."

She took a bite of her French toast and widened her eyes at me. "This is delicious."

"I told you, I always strive for excellence."

"Well, you succeeded," she said and took another bite.

I watched as she ate the food I'd cooked, and a feeling of happiness spread through me. I bit into my toast and chewed, trying to wrap my mind around the idea that I was dating now. I hadn't asked her out directly, but suddenly, I had a girlfriend. And it wasn't nearly as terrifying as I had thought it would be.

We could figure this out, I was sure of it. We just had to be careful for a while. At least until after I knew if I got the promotion or not. And a small part of me still wanted to check it out, to see if it was going to work before I made it official. A part of me still wondered if this might fail.

It wasn't fear, though. Piper deserved the benefit of the doubt.

But it was so much more complicated than whether or not we got along, whether or not we were good together.

There was my past, for one thing. My parents had tragically died when I was a young adult. As the oldest son, I'd felt responsible for my four younger brothers. I'd always had the sense that the experience of growing up quickly had somehow left me guarded and aloof. I'd avoided relationships for so long. How would I fare in a real one, at long last?

And then there was her past. She had just come out of a relationship. Her breakup had been recent, she'd said. What did that mean for us? Would it be a problem in our relationship?

I shook off the thoughts. I couldn't do this before it even had a chance to start. I was overthinking things, and I just had to let things unfold naturally.

I turned my attention back to Piper, who started telling me about a hike she was considering doing in the area. I listened to her and focused on the here and now.

This was what I wanted. She was beautiful, caring, considerate. Passionate, affectionate. This was the woman I wanted to spend time with.

This was going to be fun, exciting. How long had it been since I'd had something like that in my life?

With every single thing we took on, we took a risk. Every day at the hospital was a risk—either I saved a life or I lost it. But this risk, investing my emotions in Piper, was a risk I was sure was worth taking. We just had to take it one day at a time.

If last night had been this incredible, and this morning had continued to be incredible, there was no reason why it wouldn't stay that way.

I reached for her hand and squeezed it. She stopped in the middle of her sentence, smiled at me, and kissed me.

TWELVE

PIPER

The last thing I expected when I moved to North Haven was to find romance. I had left Roanoke because I was trying to escape a bad relationship, and I'd had no intentions of getting involved with anyone again.

When I had told Adriana that I wasn't interested in dating, I had meant it.

But Ethan was something else, and the next couple of weeks were amazing.

We kept our relationship on the downlow. It was important to him that he got that promotion, and I was happy to take things slowly at first. I didn't have to announce our relationship status to everyone around us. I was perfectly happy keeping it secret for as long as necessary.

I enjoyed seeing him, spending time with him, and learning what it was like to be in a healthy relationship. I hadn't been in a long-term relationship where the guy I was with had been self-sufficient, and it was strangely liberating to be with someone who could take care of himself. Ethan and I were together because we enjoyed each other's company, not because either of us was gaining anything from the relationship.

Because of it, I was starting to feel more and more at home, comfortable with being around him, and I felt like we were developing a real friendship. It wasn't just a relationship. It was more than that.

It had happened so fast, too.

Sometimes, I felt worried. What if it was moving too quickly? What if it was going to crash and burn because we weren't taking our time?

I spent a lot of nights at his place, and waking up next to him had become the new normal. In fact, on the odd morning that I woke up without him, I felt strangely lost and disconnected.

Ethan's behavior at work had softened a bit, too. He still demanded excellence from the staff, but his rude comments had decreased, and I no longer feared doing rotations with him. Even the other nurses had commented on his better mood.

Things were looking up.

"Come out with us for drinks tonight," Adriana said after we had lunch in the cafeteria. "I think Jeremy's interested in someone. When he gets like that, I always feed him alcohol to find out his true feelings."

I laughed. "It will be nice if he finds someone. He always seems so bothered by the fact that he's single."

"I've long stopped trying to understand him," Adriana said with a laugh. "But let's give it a shot tonight."

I shook my head. "I'm sorry, I'm going to have to take a rain check. I have a couple of things to take care of."

Adriana frowned. "Like what? You keep blowing me off. We haven't been out together in the longest time."

I nodded, feeling guilty. The truth was, I had plans with

Ethan to have dinner together and watch a movie. I could cancel on him, but I didn't want to. I couldn't get enough of him, and I couldn't explain to my friends what was going on.

"I'm just exhausted, I'm sorry," I said.

Before Adriana could respond, we were called to the ER to take care of someone coming in. I was glad for the distraction—saved by the bell, as it were. I wasn't going to be able to keep lying to Adriana forever. And I felt bad that I kept giving her excuses.

But for now, we had to keep our relationship secret.

The incident in the ER wasn't too serious, and after Adriana and I could return to our duties, she cornered me.

"Come on, Piper, you can't keep holing up in your house. It's not healthy. When you have a job like this, so emotionally taxing and physically demanding, you have to make some time to unwind. I'm putting my foot down. You're coming out with us tonight."

I hesitated. Adriana was a really good friend. Despite the fact that I was hiding my new relationship with Ethan from her, we had become quite close over the last couple of weeks. I could see that she was trying to help me. She thought I was hiding away in my house, depressed.

"Okay," I finally agreed. "I'll come out with you tonight."

She smiled at me, pleased that she had gotten what she wanted, and headed off to take care of her duties. I walked to Ethan's office and knocked on his door.

"What a surprise," he said and smiled when I walked in, closing the door behind me. He stood and walked around the desk, planting a quick kiss on my lips. It was chaste, careful, and he took a step away from me again.

"I need to talk to you about tonight," I said. "Adriana

and Jeremy insist that I go out for drinks with them, and I don't know how to lie my way out of it anymore."

Ethan smiled at me. He ran a hand down my arm, and I shivered. I loved his touch.

"Go out with them. We'll postpone our movie night. We can do it tomorrow."

"Are you sure?" I asked.

"I'm positive. You should hang out with your friends, too."

"What'll you do to keep yourself amused?" I asked.

"I'll think of something. Maybe I'll watch one of those movies you hate."

I giggled. We had an overlapping taste in movies, but there were a few I just couldn't stand.

"While I have you here, I was thinking..." Ethan started, leaning against the edge of his desk. "I don't want to keep things secret between us anymore. I think I'm going to talk to HR."

I shook my head. "You should wait."

"Why? I think things are going well between us. I don't see the need to hide any longer."

He took my hand and squeezed it as if to confirm what he had just said.

I nodded. "Things *are* going well. But I think you should wait until the promotion has been decided. There's no rush for us to make things public. We can keep it secret for a while longer."

"Are you sure?" Ethan asked. "I don't want you to think that I'm trying to hide you."

"I'm sure," I said and planted a quick kiss on his lips again. "I'll see you tomorrow. I can't wait."

"Me neither," he said, and I left his office with a smile on my face.

Adriana, Jeremy, and I sat at our usual table at the Howling Wolf. The bar was unusually full, and we had to raise our voices to hear each other above the conversations all around us and the music that blared through the speakers.

"Where have you been?" Jeremy asked as we got settled. "I hardly even recognize your face anymore."

I giggled. "You see me at work every day."

"I recognize you by your name tag there," he sniffed.

I shook my head. "I've just been trying to adjust to life here."

"You've been here long enough that this should become your new normal," Adriana pointed out.

I shrugged. "The process is different for everyone, isn't it?"

Jeremy and Adriana glanced at each other.

"We think you're seeing someone on the sly."

I gasped. "What? Who?"

Jeremy threw his hands up in the air. "We can't get that part. You're good. But we know it, and we have a theory."

"What theory?" I asked with a laugh.

Jeremy glanced at Adriana and started counting on his fingers. "You always turn us down, and you have this perpetual smile on your face like you're in love."

"He's right," Adriana agreed. "You turn down drinks from everyone who approaches you, too."

I laughed. "Just because I'm not interested in the guys at the bar, doesn't mean I'm sneaking around behind your backs."

I felt a pang of guilt as I said it. That was exactly what was happening. But I had to continue the lie for now. "I told you, I just got out of a bad relationship. I don't want to get into another one."

My friends narrowed their eyes at me, and I felt terrible that I was outright lying to them. But if they found out, the whole hospital would know tomorrow. And I couldn't do that to Ethan after I'd told him to wait before going to HR about us.

"Fine," Jeremy said. "But we're going to start getting you out of your shell, then. You need to come out with us more often. We'll have to make this a regular thing."

I couldn't argue with him. I was already making life hard for myself. I changed the subject to Jeremy's love interest, and I felt relieved to be out of the hot seat.

By the time we were finished, I was exhausted and a little tipsy. And I didn't want to go home alone. Instead, I swung by the house to make sure Charlie had food and water, and then I headed to Ethan's place. When I knocked on the door, there was no answer.

I frowned and dialed his number.

"Where are you?" I asked.

"Maybe I should ask you where you are," Ethan said, amused.

"Don't be silly. I'm outside your door."

"I'm at the neighbor's place," Ethan said. "You can come around. I was just having tea with Viola, catching up."

Ethan had mentioned Viola before, but I had never met her. Now, I wondered what it meant that he had spent time with another woman when I had been out with my friends.

I walked around to the next house, knocked on the front door, and Ethan opened.

"Hello, beautiful," he said and kissed me before stepping back. "I thought I'd come to check on Viola. She hadn't been outside in a couple of days, and I got worried."

I tried not to get jealous.

"Come on in and meet her. She doesn't feel very well, so she's not her usual bubbly self."

I followed Ethan into a house that looked decidedly old-fashioned. When I walked into the living room, I saw an elderly lady on the couch with a blanket tucked around her legs.

Oh! I quickly felt like a fool for being jealous at all.

"So, this is the girl you keep telling me about," Viola said, smiling at me. "You were right, Ethan, she is a looker."

I blushed and walked to Viola, sitting down next to her.

"Hi, I'm Piper," I said.

"I'm so glad to finally meet you," Viola said. "I hear about you all the time, you know."

I blushed, glancing at Ethan. He grinned at me before sitting down.

"I always hoped that Ethan would find someone to chase away the loneliness. Everyone needs someone, don't you think?"

"I agree," I said. "For a while, I only had my cat, and even that is better than nothing."

"I keep trying to convince him to get a puppy or something. But you are a much better option."

I giggled, and Ethan shook his head like he was a little embarrassed. If the light in the room wasn't so dim, I would have known for sure if he was blushing.

"Ethan has helped me since my husband passed away several years ago," Viola said. "My children live out of state, and Ethan has been like a son to me in many ways. He's a wonderful person. You should hold onto him, dear. I know he can seem brooding, but it's just an act."

"Oh, I know all about his act," I said and winked at Ethan.

Ethan laughed. "You shouldn't believe everything you hear about me," he said.

Viola smiled, looking from me to Ethan and back. "The two of you are beautiful together. And he likes you, that's for sure."

I blushed again, and Ethan looked uncomfortable. But Viola didn't seem to mince her words. She said what she thought, and I liked that about her.

Besides, knowing that Ethan felt something for me excited me. I had strong feelings for him, too. I was starting to fall for him. I was getting attached. I couldn't exactly call it love. Something like that had to grow over time. But I knew that I liked spending time with him and being here tonight was evidence of that.

I didn't want to be without him anymore.

When I glanced at Ethan again, his eyes were soft, and his lips curled in a smile. He cared about Viola, and I saw a side of him that I knew he rarely showed anyone else. At the hospital, he was often gruff and unapproachable. But when he wasn't at the hospital, when we were all alone, and the world wasn't watching, I saw the side of him that I was falling for. And now, hearing how he had been helping Viola all these years, I was starting to see through his facade to see the man he truly was.

And I couldn't find a single fault that would change my mind about where we were headed.

THIRTEEN

PIPER

"You don't have to be so nervous," Ethan said, standing behind me and rubbing my shoulders.

I stood in front of the mirror, trying to decide if what I was wearing was too formal.

I had put on a pair of black pants and a white blouse, and now it all felt too stark.

"Maybe I should put on something else," I said.

"They are going to love you," Ethan said.

"How do you know that?" I asked, looking at the selection of outfits I had laid out on Ethan's bed. I had brought a lot of clothes to his place this time, terrified that I would make the wrong first impression on his brother and sister-in-law.

I hadn't met any of Ethan's family yet. Gavin was Ethan's second brother, and he was newly married to Jolie. I had heard a lot about his brothers, but in the spirit of keeping our relationship a secret, we had only spent time with each other.

Tonight, we were finally going to have dinner at Gavin's

house, and I was terrified that there would be some reason why they wouldn't like me, a reason for them to tell Ethan I wasn't girlfriend material.

"Because I'm crazy about you, and they'll be happy to know I'm happy."

I nodded, but I was still panicked. Ethan wrapped his arms around me and folded me against his body, holding me tightly.

"Relax, it's going to be okay."

After changing my outfit one more time—I finally selected a summery pastel dress that was a lot more casual and colorful than the outfit I had chosen before—Ethan and I drove to Gavin and Jolie's place.

They lived in a stunning house on the other side of town, and Gavin came out to greet us.

"It's nice to finally meet you," he said, pulling me into a hug even though I had only offered my hand. "We've all been secretly taking bets on when Ethan would finally find someone."

"Don't be an ass," Ethan laughed.

"Really?" I asked, surprised.

Ethan punched Gavin lightly in the shoulder, and the two brothers laughed. It was clear that they were close. With five brothers, I could imagine that things could get interesting. Seeing how he was around Gavin just gave me more insight into who Ethan was behind his gruff exterior.

We walked into the house, and I was introduced to Jolie.

She was just as kind and welcoming as Gavin, and I felt at home right away. I realized why Ethan had said I didn't have to worry about meeting them. Everything about them was wonderful.

We sat down around the large dining table, and the conversation flowed comfortably.

"Has he shouted at you at the hospital yet?" Gavin asked.

I glanced at Ethan. "Only about a dozen times," I said.

Gavin laughed, and Ethan shook his head.

"It's business," Ethan protested. "It's not a game. People can die."

I giggled and Gavin winked at me.

"We're just messing with you, bro. You're doing something right if Piper is still around."

Gavin waggled his eyebrows at me, and I giggled again.

The two brothers continued to banter back and forth, and I watched the interaction. Ethan was so kind and caring around his family, it was difficult to bring these two people together—the man he was at the hospital and the man he was away from work.

What had caused him to be this way?

After supper, I helped Jolie in the kitchen. The guys had cooked the meal, so we were on clean-up duty.

"I thought he was very sullen when I met him at first," Jolie admitted while she washed the dishes and I dried them off. "But after a while, when he warms up to you, he's a completely different person."

"Yeah, I've noticed that," I said. "He's a saint to me as long as we're not in the ER. But he's right... It is a matter of life and death."

Jolie smiled. "He's really into you."

"Really?" I asked. "You're not the first person to say that."

Jolie nodded. "I've never seen Ethan with anyone. He's always so closed off and distant. He doesn't easily get attached. You should feel honored."

I *did* feel honored. But I felt like there was a part of Ethan I still didn't understand. I had a feeling that his parents' death had impacted him a lot worse than I initially thought.

"Was Gavin the same when you just met?" I asked.

"Not at all," Jolie said after thinking about it for a moment. "But then, I met Gavin when we were kids, long before their parents were killed." She put the dish down and sighed. "Their deaths were hard on all those brothers, and they each handled it in their own way."

I nodded, and she continued.

"We've had our problems, Gavin and me, and we got through it. That's one thing the Coles have in common. They will fight for what they believe in. Ethan is very caring, and he will make sure that things work out."

I nodded, wondering about Gavin and Jolie's relationship. They seemed so connected now, it was difficult to imagine that they had problems. I hoped that we wouldn't run into trouble. But with how perfect everything was now, it was difficult to believe anything could go wrong.

"You won't tell anyone about our relationship, will you?" I asked. "I want Ethan to have a shot at the promotion before we go public with it."

"You don't have to worry about us," Jolie said with a smile. "Ethan already told Gavin that you're keeping it quiet for now, and we're not exactly the types to go blabbing to everyone. We've both had our fill of small-town gossip."

"That's refreshing. It seems like everyone around here is in everyone else's business."

Jolie laughed. "It's one of the perks of living in a small town, isn't it? You know everything about everyone. And everyone knows everything about you, too."

I shook my head, smiling. "It's something to get used to.

But luckily, once Ethan's job selection is over, I'll have nothing to hide."

We finished up in the kitchen, and Jolie made everyone coffee before we walked to the living room where the guys were talking, laughing, and bantering back and forth. When Ethan looked at me, his eyes filled with affection, and I believed what Jolie had said with my whole heart.

If he wanted something, he would make it work.

And he wanted me.

In the car on the way back home, Ethan glanced at me.

"How was it?" he asked.

"Great," I said to him with a smile, and he grinned at me. "I liked them a lot."

"I'm glad," he said and slid his hand onto my thigh. "I was nervous."

"You didn't look nervous at all." I thought about it. "I don't know that I've *ever* seen you nervous."

He laughed. "I was nervous going over to your house to apologize that day."

"Could've fooled me," I laughed. He always seemed so confident and self-assured.

"I'm happy you had a good time," he said. "It means a lot to me that you liked my family."

I smiled and looked out of the window at a sleepy North Haven passing by.

When we pulled up in front of Ethan's house, we climbed out and walked in together. Ethan closed the front door and turned to me.

"It also means a lot to me that you came with me tonight."

"I like that you want to introduce me to your family," I said.

Ethan cupped my cheek and kissed me, sliding his

tongue over my lips, and I parted my lips and let him in. He tugged at my lip and kissed me again, tasting, exploring.

Our tongues swirled slowly around each other as I lost myself in him. I loved the way he kissed me, touched me.

His hands roamed my body. I leaned against him, feeling his erection press against me.

I ran my hands over his shoulders, his back, down his arms.

Ethan pushed my dress up, his hands on my breasts, and I moaned into his mouth when he squeezed. I lifted my arms, and he pulled my dress over my head.

I lifted his shirt off him, and he removed my bra. I pushed my breasts against his chest, his skin warm.

He slid his hands to cup my ass, squeezing it through my lace underwear.

I sank to my knees in front of Ethan, and he smiled down at me.

"I love it when you do that," he said.

I looked up at him while I pulled his cock free from his jeans. "I love doing it, too."

Ethan's cock was hard, the skin smooth, silk over steel, and I rubbed my hand over it a few times before I sucked his head into my mouth. He groaned when I swirled my tongue around his shaft, pushing my head forward, sucking him deeper into my mouth. I pulled his pants down far enough that he was practically naked in front of me and cupped his balls.

Ethan grunted and pushed his hands into my hair. He encouraged me to suck harder and faster, and I started bobbing my head back and forth. His grunts and moans were such a turn-on.

"God, you're going to push me to the edge before I get to do anything," he complained, his voice breathy.

I pulled back and chuckled at him.

He held out his hand, and I took it. Ethan pulled me up and we walked to the bedroom together, touching, kissing along the way. I wanted him. Not just because I was horny as hell, but because I wanted to be close to him, connected to him.

As soon as we were in the bedroom, Ethan kissed me again, and we collapsed on the bed. He kissed me on the lips gently, running his hand along my cheek, down my neck, and onto my shoulder.

The atmosphere shifted, and where it had been about sex a moment ago, about being turned on and getting off, it was completely emotional now. Ethan's eyes were intense in the dark when he broke the kiss, his face only inches away from mine. I could feel his hot breath on my skin.

His hand slid down to my breasts, my nipples hard, standing at attention, begging for Ethan to touch them.

He ground himself against me, his hard cock pressing into my pelvis when he cupped my breasts.

He squeezed them gently and teased my nipples.

"Do you have any idea how beautiful you are?" he asked.

"I know how you make me feel," I whispered.

Ethan moved to my breasts and started kissing my nipples, sucking on them. His hand roamed my stomach, sliding further and further down until he cupped my pussy.

I was soaking wet for him. I needed his touch desperately.

I slid my hand down his body and cupped his cock, hard and hot against my hip. I ran my fingers over him, and he groaned. He moved his lips back to mine, and I opened my mouth, sucking his tongue into my mouth. We held onto each other, sucking and kissing and holding each other tightly.

"I want you inside of me," I murmured between kisses. I was getting wetter. I needed him to fill me. I ached for him.

Ethan moved his hand and caressed my breasts again, kissing his way down my neck and over my chest. Slowly, he worked his way down my body, and I opened my legs for him. I moaned when he closed his mouth over me, licking my clit, and I squirmed and bucked my hips.

He didn't stay down there to push me to orgasm. Instead, he just teased me until I couldn't take it anymore, keeping me on the verge of an orgasm before he backed away.

I moaned in protest.

"Please," I whispered.

I wanted him to make me orgasm.

Instead, he crawled over me again and pushed into me. He must have slipped on a condom at some point, although I hadn't heard him do it. But the feel of him was incredible.

The motion was smooth, and his cock was suddenly inside me, filling me up. I cried out when he split me open, and I shivered around him, breathing hard when I looked up at him.

His face was riddled with a mixture of lust and need and affection, and his eyes locked on mine when he started thrusting. Slowly and sensually at first, moving in and out of me as he looked me in the eyes.

I breathed harder, his rhythm pushing the air out of my lungs and letting it back in.

Slowly, he started thrusting inside me harder and harder.

I felt connected to him in a way I'd never felt before.

Ethan pumped into me harder and harder, his breathing getting faster, and I shivered and cried out as he pushed me closer and closer again to the orgasm he had started a moment ago. The closer I came, the louder I moaned and cried out.

Ethan was getting closer, too. I could feel it, his cock rock hard inside of me and the rhythm of his thrusts changing.

I felt like I was filling up, warm water spilling through my body until I was so full, I spilled over. I cried out as the orgasm washed through me.

As if it pushed him over the edge, too, he barked a cry and I felt him pulsate inside of me where he was buried as deep as he could go.

We orgasmed together, and the sensation was like nothing I had ever experienced before.

When it was over, he collapsed on me, and we lay there, chests heaving against each other as we relearned how to breathe. Eventually, he rolled off me, but we were still so tightly pressed up against each other, it was hard to tell where I ended and he began.

He pulled me tightly against him, his arm pulling me even closer, lips against my ear.

"I'm crazy about you," he whispered.

"I feel the same," I answered.

"Stay the night?" he asked.

I nodded. It wasn't even a question I needed to think about. I'd been planning to stay anyway.

But knowing that it was what he wanted, as well, made me feel wanted.

He made me feel incredible.

How had I gotten so lucky that I'd ended up with such an amazing man? After years and years of being treated like shit, I was with a man who treated me like I was his everything.

He treated me like a queen.

It was impossible not to fall for him. But I knew falling wasn't dangerous. Not this time.

Because no matter what, he was going to catch me.

FOURTEEN

PIPER

I was late for work. Ethan had come over to my place last night, and we'd had a wonderful time. He hadn't stayed over, though. Instead, he'd left after dinner and an intense session in the bedroom so that he could prepare for a review at work.

I had overslept, not hearing my alarm at all.

"Shit, shit, shit," I muttered as I scrambled across my room, trying to get everything together.

I looked for a hair tie to pull back my hair, but I couldn't find one. I ran into the bathroom, yanked open the cabinet, and searched. I knocked over a couple of things in the process, and a box of tampons fell on the floor, the tampons scattering across the tiles.

"Dammit," I breathed and sank to my knees to scrape the tampons together.

I frowned while I stuffed them back in the box. Suddenly, it felt like too long since I had used my tampons. Wasn't I supposed to be on my period again?

I sat back on my heels and tried to calculate the days. When had my last period been? I tried to anchor it to something else that had happened in my life so that I could remember the dates.

Charlie came into the bathroom, meowing at me for his food.

"This can't be right, can it?" I asked him, ignoring his pleas. I tried to calculate again, and again, I came to the same conclusion.

My period was over two weeks late.

I didn't have a lot of time to worry about it. I wasn't at the hospital on time, and I was going to get in trouble. It wasn't the first time I'd been late. Sometimes, Ethan and I couldn't get enough of each other, and I arrived at the hospital frazzled and flushed.

It was probably nothing, anyway. I didn't have to worry about it. My period wasn't always regular. It had been a little late in the past, and everything had been fine.

"You look stressed out," Adriana said when I ran into the locker room and threw my bag into my cubicle.

"I overslept," I said.

She chuckled. "It's been happening a lot more lately. What are you doing that's keeping you up so late?"

I fought the urge to blush. "Oh, you know how it goes. Sometimes I scroll social media until all hours of the morning."

"Tell me about it," Jeremy said, joining us. "You open social media, and before you know it, four hours have passed, and you don't know what you've done with your life."

Adriana shook her head. "Am I the only one without that problem?"

"It's not a bad thing to be different," Jeremy said with a roll of his eyes. "Trust me, social media is a demon."

Adriana and I giggled, and we got to doing our rounds,

waking up patients and administering the medication before the doctors did their rounds much later.

Despite the demands of my work, I couldn't stop thinking about the fact that my period was late. I was starting to worry about it. My stomach was twisted in a tight knot of nerves, and I kept trying to convince myself it wasn't a big deal. I'd had a pregnancy scare with Chris once, too. Two weeks late, just like this time. And just when I had wanted to tell him that we might have a problem, my period had started.

Besides, Ethan and I were always careful. He always used condoms. Without exception.

Suddenly, I remembered that one night. We had been out to dinner together, having driven to another town so that we could go out in public without being recognized. It had been fantastic—one of the best nights we'd had so far.

By the time we had made it home, we hadn't had any condoms.

"It will be fine," I had said to him.

"I can go out and get some," he'd offered.

But we had both been riddled with lust, aching for each other, unwilling to break the spell, and after a quick calculation, I had figured it was an infertile day.

Had I been wrong?

I couldn't do this right now. A baby? I was focusing on my career. It had been about three months since I had moved to North Haven, but I was still new here, and I wanted to make my mark. Not to mention the fact that Ethan and I weren't as serious as starting a family together. Not yet.

I wished I could talk to someone about it. But who?

I couldn't tell Adriana or Jeremy about my worries without them finding out about Ethan. And since I hadn't told my parents back home about any of it either, the conversation would come as a bit of a shock. I didn't feel like all the explanations that would have to follow.

No, I decided, the easiest way would be for me to keep quiet for now. I'd go to the store after work and take a test. It would probably be negative anyway. And then I would have worried for nothing.

When I knocked off work, turning down Adriana for an impromptu movie night, I made my way to the store. I walked to the aisle where the pregnancy tests hung in a row —right next to the condoms as if in ironic reproach. And the baby products on the other side—diapers, bottles, pacifiers.

This was what happened, it seemed to scream at me, if you were irresponsible.

I shook my head and took two tests off the shelf. When I walked with them to the counter, I felt like everyone was staring at me. My fingers trembled when I took money out of my purse, and I worried that the people around me were whispering about me.

Did they know who I was? Did they know what was happening? Surely, the cashier would put two and two together. And if any one of them had been admitted to the hospital recently, they might recognize my face.

Just keep it together, I told myself softly after paying and leaving the store.

When I got home, Charlie came to greet me.

"The move here has been nothing but crazy," I told him when I picked him up to cuddle him. "Sometimes, I think I've grown up and I won't get myself into a mess anymore. And then, just like that, here we are again."

Charlie purred when I scratched him between the ears. I carried him to my bedroom and put him down on the bed before I walked into the bathroom. I took a deep breath, read the instructions on the pregnancy test box three times, and did what I needed to do.

Two minutes. That was how long I'd have to wait for the results.

Two minutes were nothing. Unless the rest of your life hinged on those two minutes. Then, they felt like a lifetime.

When the time was finally over, I picked up the test stick from the counter where I had put it.

My heart beat in my throat. I felt lightheaded, dizzy. I squeezed my eyes shut, covering the test window with my thumb.

Charlie sat in the door to the bathroom, watching me with his amber eyes.

"Let's hope, kitten," I said to him, the way I used to talk to him when he was just a baby.

I looked at the test and moved my thumb. And gasped for breath. My stomach sank. I sat down on the edge of the tub, and my eyes welled up with tears.

Pregnant.

I was pregnant. One night without a condom, and this happened. What the hell? Wasn't I going to get a break?

I threw the test in the trash can—as if that would make any difference—and covered my face with my hands. My shoulders shook as I cried, the tension of the day flowing out now that no one was watching and I didn't have a reason to keep it together anymore.

What was I going to do? I'd always wanted kids, but I never pictured it this way. Ethan and I weren't serious yet. We spent a lot of time together, and I loved being with him, but it hadn't been that long. Plus, we were still keeping our relationship a secret. It wasn't exactly the most ideal situation to raise a family in.

No one knew we were together. Only Gavin and Jolie.

God, what was I even going to say? How would he take it? He had a career, too. And he was as casual about our relationship as I was. Three months wasn't a lot of time together. Definitely not enough to know that we wanted to do this for the rest of our lives. And now? Raising a child together wasn't a joke.

And what if we weren't together? What if I had to do it all alone?

My emotions crashed down on me, and I struggled to see the light.

I had to tell him. I had to get this out in the open as soon as possible, or I wasn't going to be able to get through this. As long as I knew what was happening, maybe I could find a way to deal with it. But there was too much uncertainty right now.

I wanted to tell Ethan right away, but when I called him to ask if I could come over, he was busy at the hospital and I only got his voicemail. And the next night, I would be on the evening shift, working until well after midnight.

As much as we saw each other sometimes, there were weeks where we didn't get to see each other at all, and this was one of them. It was a whole week before it finally got to a point where Ethan and I could spend time together again.

When I went to his house for dinner, I felt sick to my stomach. Morning sickness? Maybe not yet.

Nerves, panic.

I didn't know how he was going to react. I didn't know what he would say.

"Are you okay?" Ethan asked after we sat down. "You look like you don't feel very well."

"I don't," I admitted. I took a deep breath. I had to tell him.

Here goes.

"I don't feel well, either," Ethan said, and I blinked at him.

"What's wrong?" I asked carefully.

He took a deep breath and let it out slowly. "I don't usually talk about these things, but the truth is... Today is the anniversary of my parents' death."

I gasped. I'd had no idea it was such a difficult day for him. Telling him about my pregnancy on a day like today wasn't going to go down very well.

"Oh, sweetie, I'm so sorry," I said, putting my arm around his shoulders.

"A damned drunk driver took their lives. He killed my parents, and he walked away from the scene without a scratch." Ethan shook his head. "These things happen, don't they? It's not like I was a kid when we lost them. Sometimes, I feel like I should be able to deal with it by now."

"Death doesn't get any easier the further we move away from it," I said softly. "We just become better at handling it from time to time. It's okay not to be okay."

"Is it weird to say that I'm angry at them?" Ethan asked.

"I don't think it's weird. Why are you angry?" I asked, settling into the fact that I wasn't going to be able to speak to him about the pregnancy tonight. It was not the right time to tell him he was going to be a father. My news could wait another day.

"I know it wasn't their fault. And I guess I'm not angry at them, exactly. I just feel like it's unfair I had to take on so much responsibility so early in life. Sometimes, I wish things had been different. And I miss them, Piper. I miss them so much."

I pulled him closer into an embrace. I felt so bad for him, and I hated the fact that he had to go through all of this.

Ethan told me more about his parents. His dad had been a distant father to his five sons and a cutthroat businessman. He'd had a reputation as a greedy miser in the town. The brothers had resented him for his callous treatment of them, and when he'd passed, they'd each struggled with their own guilt and anger over their difficult relationship with him.

In contrast, their mother had been loving to the boys. Their grief for her was less complicated but even more raw. Together, the two losses devastated the five sons.

As the oldest and in his early twenties at the time, Ethan had been thrust into the harsh reality of responsibility too early. Though their grandmother gained custody of the three youngest brothers until they'd each turned eighteen, Ethan had still carried the weight of looking after them in many ways. He'd quickly become a father figure to them, striving to do better than his own father had done with him.

Gradually, I began to understand Ethan's hardened front he showed to the world. He'd had to be so strong for everyone at a young age. He could never show a weakness. Over time, he'd built a wall around himself.

Listening to his story only made me respect and admire him all the more.

"I appreciate that you're here for me, Piper," Ethan said toward the end of the night when we'd talked through dinner and coffee afterward. "I've never really been able to open up about all this. I can't talk to my brothers about it because we're all hurting in one way or another. Sometimes, it only makes it worse to bring it up. This is the first time I've talked to someone who can understand."

I squeezed his hand. "I'll always be here for you to talk to," I said.

He smiled at me gratefully, his eyes locked on mine.

Later, I lay beside him in bed, listening to him breathe deeply in his sleep. I was wide awake, worries filling my mind as I stared into the darkness.

I'll always be here for you, I'd told him.

Would the opposite be true? Would Ethan be there for me when he found out he was going to be a father?

FIFTEEN

ETHAN

A nagging feeling tugged at me.

The last couple of days, Piper was different. A little distant. Scattered even.

I was worried she was pulling away from me.

It had all started shortly after the time we'd had dinner with Gavin and Jolie.

Had it been too much? Should I have waited before introducing her to one of my brothers? I was starting to worry that maybe she hadn't been ready for it.

But surely, she would have said something. After all, Piper wasn't the type to keep things quiet. If she thought something, she said it. She was outspoken, albeit diplomatic. It was something that I loved about her.

Maybe her problem was with me. What if I had done something wrong?

It was almost a week later when I finally caught her alone at work. She was at the nurses' station taking care of the paperwork. It was almost midnight, and everyone else had gone home or was tending to patients.

I had only stopped working now, as there had been a lot of paperwork for me to take care of.

"Hey," I said. When she looked up at me, she withdrew. Her eyes became guarded. "Are you okay?"

"Perfectly fine," she said with a smile that didn't reach her eyes. "I love working night shift."

"I know," I said. "There's something about being alone here."

She smiled at me again and nodded. There was a small spark between us, something that resembled our usual connection. But it slipped away almost immediately again.

"Are you sure everything is okay?" I asked. When she frowned slightly, I continued. "I mean between us."

Piper glanced around as if someone would overhear us, but it was only the two of us in a very long, very empty corridor.

"We're fine," she said.

"If something is bothering you, you know you can tell me, right?"

She nodded without hesitation. "I know. I just have a lot to deal with right now. Work sometimes gets to me."

I nodded. It wasn't always easy to be a nurse or a doctor. We saved lives, but sometimes we lost them, too. And we had lost one that week. I knew that Piper became emotionally attached to the patients in some way. Not so much that it would affect her job, but it still affected her personally. Maybe that was what I was seeing.

But if she didn't want to talk to me about it, there was nothing I could do.

"Are you ready for the fundraiser this weekend?" I asked, deciding to mention the black-tie hospital fundraiser as I stalled for time. "I hate that we can't go together."

"Yeah, that's too bad," she said. "But it'll be nice to do something formal. I like the idea of dressing up."

I nodded. I liked the idea of us dressing up, too.

"Well, I'll see you tomorrow," I said. I wanted to add that she could talk to me about anything, but I'd already said it, and I didn't want to look as worried as I felt.

I turned around and walked away from her, fighting the urge to look back over my shoulder.

The rest of the week passed in a blur, and before I knew it, I had to get ready for the fundraiser. I dressed in a tuxedo I had sent to the dry cleaners earlier in the week and looked at myself in the mirror.

Not bad. Not bad at all.

It had been a while since I'd had a reason to dress up like this, and I was looking forward to seeing Piper.

When I arrived, I mingled with the other doctors, making small talk, waiting for Piper to arrive. Finally, when she did, she walked into the large room with Adriana and one of the male nurses.

I'd been having a conversation with one of the other doctors, but I stopped listening to what he was saying, suddenly unable to concentrate on anything but Piper. It was like the whole world fell away, and she stood in the middle of the room, iridescent, an angel.

She had put on a red satin dress that clung to her curves, with a low neck and a slit to her thigh. She wore black strappy heels with it, and her hair had been curled into an elegant updo. She had put on smoky eye make-up, and everything about her was perfect.

But her expression didn't suit the clothes she wore. Something about her seemed off. She looked sad, as if something were very wrong.

That feeling of worry in my gut got tighter.

"Ethan?" someone asked behind me, and I turned to see Nate. He had already removed his blazer and rolled up his sleeves, with his hands casually in his pockets. "I haven't seen you in ages. I thought you might have died."

"In our line of work, that's not such a funny joke," I said.

Nathan chuckled. "Yeah, I guess not. What are you staring at?"

"The nurses," I said.

Nate and I turned back to the nurses. I stared at Piper, specifically. Nate took in the rest of them.

Nate whistled through his teeth. "We should do fundraisers like this more often. The gals at work aren't very hot in their scrubs, but like this... It makes me see them in a new light."

"It makes you look at them in the first place," I said with a chuckle.

"True. Well, I'm going to get a drink, and then I'm going to chat one of them up," he said. "Join me?"

I shook my head. "I think I'm going to mingle a little more around here."

Nate rolled his eyes. "Not everything has to be about business, you know."

He was right, it didn't have to be. And for me, it wouldn't be. I wasn't going to mingle with other doctors. I wanted to talk to Piper. Alone.

I spotted her a short while later, standing to the side of the crowd, looking a little lost. I walked to her.

When she saw me, her eyes trailed me, but her face remained serious.

"You don't look like you're having a lot of fun," I said.

She shrugged. "I don't think I belong in a setting like this."

"So, run away with me," I suggested.

She looked up at me, her eyes sparkling for the first time in a while. "What?"

"Let's get out of here and go back to my place."

"Aren't we supposed to be here for the good of the hospital?"

I glanced around at the other doctors and nurses and administrative staff. "They're doing the hospital plenty of good without us. If we sneak away now, I doubt anyone will miss us."

Piper giggled. "Okay," she said, nodding.

Her agreement came as a bit of a surprise. I had half-expected her to turn me down. Whatever was bugging her, I had started to become convinced that it was me.

But now that she was so eager to spend time with me alone, I took the opportunity. We slipped out through a side door, and I grabbed her hand when we were alone. We were laughing when we finally reached my car, and I drove us back to my place.

"This is much better," Piper said when we climbed out of the car and walked to the front door. "This dress is beautiful, but I can't wait to get out of it."

"You're telling *me*," I said with a smile.

But as soon as we were inside, that sad expression returned to her perfect face. I frowned at her, hooking a stray hair behind her ear.

"Are you sure you're okay?" I asked. "You look like something is getting to you."

"I'm just tired," she said.

I nodded. She'd been working the night shift for the past two weeks, and it made sense that she was exhausted.

"We can just go to bed if you want?" I asked.

"Oh, I want to go to bed, all right. But what I have in mind doesn't involve much sleeping."

I chuckled and kissed her. Piper was special. She made everything feel like an adventure. Sometimes, her jokes surprised me: witty, with a touch of something endearing, something almost dirty. But she was so elegant at the same time. The fact that she was incredible in bed was icing on the cake.

She threw her arms around my neck when we kissed and pushed her body against mine.

I'd missed her. Piper had been so distant that it felt like I almost hadn't seen her. But now, she was back. In my arms where she belonged. As she kissed me, I could tell she was back with me mentally and emotionally, too.

I ran my hands over her body, and she moaned softly. Our rhythm together came to us naturally now. The way she sounded and moved when I touched her was familiar. We had fallen into a stride with each other, and it made me not want to be with anyone else again.

Once upon a time, I had been fine with one-night stands. I'd preferred to be with a different woman each time. But now that I had Piper, and everything between us was so comfortable, I didn't want to go back to sex with a stranger.

I ran my hand down her open back, feeling her skin under my fingertips, and she sighed softly. I pulled her tightly against me and ground my body against her, letting her feel how hard I was, how badly I wanted her.

She nibbled on my lower lip, and I groaned. I started peeling the dress off her. It looked incredible, but I was sure it would look better on my floor. She ran her hand up the inside of my thigh, still kissing me, and finally, she grasped my erection.

I pulled away from her and led her to my bedroom. I

wanted us somewhere comfortable where I could get lost in her.

When we were in the room, she stepped out of her dress that I'd undone halfway. She unhooked her bra and stood before me naked except for her panties.

Her breasts were perfect, with her nipples erect. I dipped my head and sucked the left one into my mouth while I massaged her right breast. I scraped my teeth gently over her nipple, and she moaned and sighed in response.

God, the sound of her moaning was incredible. It made me hot for her. I wanted to be inside of her. I wanted to be closer to her again.

I moved my mouth to her other nipple and slid my hand over her flat stomach. When I pushed it into her panties, she opened her legs a little, widening her stance, and I pushed my fingers into her slit. She was wet.

"You feel fantastic," I whispered.

She moaned when I pushed my fingers into her, pulling the sheer material of her panties away. She started moving her hips, and I retrieved my fingers and started teasing her clit, flicking my fingers back and forth over it.

Her breathing became shallow, and she trembled and whimpered as she neared an orgasm.

I loved it when she orgasmed. I loved watching her fall apart, becoming the most raw and vulnerable version of herself.

When she came, she bucked her hips against my fingers, gripping my arms tightly as she gasped and moaned. She leaned her forehead against my chest and shuddered.

I smiled and dropped a kiss in her hair.

"How does this always happen?" she asked in a breathy voice, looking up at me. Her cheeks were flushed, and her eyes were bright.

"What?" I asked with a chuckle.

"That you're still dressed when I'm practically naked."

I smiled at her and started unbuttoning my shirt, getting rid of my jacket, my pants, all of it. I was always so focused on her, my needs came much later.

She pulled off her panties, and then we were naked together.

I found a condom in my nightstand drawer and wrapped up my cock. She glanced at me, an expression on her face that I didn't quite understand.

I pulled her close in a kiss, and she melted against me.

When we fell onto the bed together, Piper took charge right away. She pushed me backward so that I lay on my back and straddled me.

She sank onto me without ceremony, crying out when she did, her head tilted back, lips parted, hands braced on my chest to keep herself upright. I ran my hands over her thighs, gripping her hips, and when she started rocking back and forth, her moans long and slow, I groaned, the feeling of pure sexual bliss washing through me.

She started riding me harder and harder, moaning as she bucked her hips, my cock sliding in and out of her. She was working on another orgasm. I could see it by the way her brows knit together and she bit her bottom lip.

I'd had other positions in mind, but she was pushing me closer to the edge as well, bringing on an orgasm a lot quicker than I'd expected.

I gripped her hips harder, pulling her forward so that I drove deeper and pushing her back again so that I slid out of her. We built a rhythm that was hard and fast, and her face contorted with pleasure, her lips parted and her breath coming in ragged gasps and moans.

We fucked harder and harder until my cock throbbed so

hard, I could take no more. Pleasure exploded at my core, and I shoved myself into her as deep as I could, releasing. I pulsated inside of her, and she moaned and cried out as my release pushed her over the edge into orgasm as well.

She collapsed onto my chest, shuddering and trembling, moans and whimpers escaping her mouth. I wrapped my arms around her, jerking and pulsing with the last of my orgasm before I started to calm down, catching my breath.

I wanted her to stay on top of me like this, connected and close, but she rolled off me, pushing out of my arms. When she lay down next to me, she pulled her knees higher up, a barrier between us, and curled her arms against her chest.

"Are you okay?" I asked.

"Perfect," she said with a smile.

I smiled at her, but I wasn't so sure I believed her. She closed her eyes, shutting me out, and I had no idea how to reach her.

What was happening? Everything had been so great, and now it felt like she was slipping through my fingers.

SIXTEEN

PIPER

At some point, I was going to have to tell him about the baby. It had been two weeks since I had found out I was pregnant, and I still hadn't managed to find a way to tell him.

So, tonight was the night. No more postponing. No more finding excuses to keep it a secret. There were too many secrets already.

It was a few days after the fundraiser, and Ethan and I were having a date night.

I was the one who had asked for it. If I didn't do it now, I might never find the nerve to tell him what was going on.

He was coming to my place for the date night, and I had cleaned up, bought some flowers for the dining room table which we never used, and found a recipe online that I was trying. I didn't usually cook.

"Well, this looks amazing," Ethan said when he stepped in. "The dining room table?"

I nodded. "A little more romantic than eating at the breakfast nook every day, isn't it?"

He smiled and pulled me closer for a kiss. "Definitely."

"I made lasagna, too."

Ethan looked surprised.

"And a salad."

He chuckled. "Pasta and a salad. Why does that sound familiar?"

I blushed, feeling silly when I realized that it was very similar to our first meal together. But this pasta dish was a lot better, and I had gone out of my way to make an exotic salad.

"So, what's the special occasion?" Ethan asked.

"Special? I just thought it would be nice if we did something different than usual."

My stomach twisted. Of course, it wasn't just the fact that I was trying to be romantic. But I couldn't very well blurt it out that I was pregnant right now, could I?

We sat down after I dished it out for us, and Ethan took a bite.

"Did you make this from scratch?" he asked, pointing at the food with his fork.

I froze, looking at him. Was it horrible?

"I'm not much of a cook," I said.

Ethan shook his head. "It's incredible. I can't believe you made this."

I gasped. "Really?" I took a bite of my food and leaned back in my chair, chewing.

God, it was good. Apparently, I knew how to cook, I just didn't know it.

"The recipe was foolproof, I have to admit," I said.

Ethan chuckled and continued eating.

I hesitated, trying to think of how I was going to introduce the topic. I didn't want to come right out and say it.

I'm pregnant.

I doubted it was going to go down well.

"I was thinking about your family," I started.

"Yeah?" Ethan asked, looking unsure about where the conversation was going. Well, that made two of us. I had no idea how to bring this around.

"You said you have a niece, right? Maisy?"

Ethan nodded, spearing a piece of lettuce and popping it into his mouth. "She's a sweetheart," he said. "You'll meet her, at some point."

"I'd like that," I said. "Is she the only child?"

"Do you mean in the family? Yeah. None of my other brothers have children. And I think it's going to stay that way for a while."

"You all seem to be so open to family," I said carefully, navigating my way through the darkness.

"Sure," Ethan said. "I guess losing our parents made us want families. We all have issues because they passed away, of course, but when it comes to family, nothing is more important."

"That's beautiful," I said. "I can just imagine what Christmas and Thanksgiving would look like with so many children running around one day."

Ethan chuckled. "It's nothing more than a fantasy right now."

"Why?"

I took another bite of my lasagna, eyeing Ethan, hoping that he was going to guide this conversation in the right direction without knowing it.

"Because I don't want any children."

I froze, blinking at him.

"What?"

He set his fork down. "I guess it's good we're having this conversation now. You might as well know how I feel about it. I love Maisy with all my heart, but I don't have time for children. I want to focus on my career. I can't handle more responsibility, not now. I've had responsibility for my entire adult life."

My stomach dropped, and I felt cold. I carefully put my fork down.

"I think it would be different if you have children, though," I said. "You share the responsibility with someone else, after all."

Ethan nodded. "Raising kids is crazy. I've seen what my brother Owen has been through with Maisy. You have to make so many sacrifices. And I've already sacrificed a lot. My brothers are all safe and sound now, and I can finally sit back and relax. I don't want to ruin that by having children."

I nodded and looked down at my plate, my appetite gone. I was starting to feel a little sick.

"Does that bother you?" Ethan asked.

When I looked up at him, he was concerned.

"No," I said quickly. "If that's how you feel about it, I can't tell you to be different."

"But we're together. This might become an issue for you at some point."

I pulled up a shoulder, trying to look nonchalant. "We've only been together a short while, right? It's not something we're looking at right now."

God, the words were falling out of my mouth without me knowing exactly what I was saying. What was I going to do? He didn't want children. If I told him right now that I was carrying his child, he was going to reject me.

I couldn't tell him. How would I?

But he would find out at some point, wouldn't he? I wasn't going to be able to hide it forever.

Still, that wasn't going to be right away. I would figure out a way to do it. I just had to think about how to approach it right.

The rest of the dinner was awkward. I tried to make conversation, to smile and laugh and talk about mundane things. But my emotions were a mess. I didn't know what I was going to do, and every time I thought about having to raise this baby on my own, about losing Ethan, I wanted to cry.

Ethan was starting to see that something was wrong. He didn't know what. I tried to tell him that everything was fine. But he wasn't stupid, and he could tell that something between us had changed. We had been so good together for several weeks, but it wasn't that simple now.

By the time the date was over, I was exhausted, physically and emotionally.

I was relieved when Ethan offered to go home instead of staying over.

"I know you have a lot on your plate, so I'm going to let you get a good night's sleep," he said. He kissed me.

I nodded. "Thank you for coming over. I had a great time."

He smiled. "I always have a great time with you."

When he left, I closed the door and sagged against it. Charlie jumped onto the couch and watched me, tail twitching.

"How would *you* have done it?" I asked him. "You have it so much easier, and you don't even know it."

I walked to my bedroom, stripped off my clothes, and climbed in between the sheets, naked. I switched off the bedroom lights and lay in the darkness, trying not to fall apart.

For a moment, I considered calling my mom. But what was I going to say to her?

Hey, Mom, guess what? I'm pregnant!

She didn't even know I was dating. I hadn't wanted to tell my parents about Ethan because it was so soon after Chris. I had given them a whole speech about how moving to North Haven would be a breakaway, a fresh start where I could be myself without anyone involved.

Having to tell them that I had gotten involved with someone right away was one thing. To tell them that I was now pregnant was another.

And my mom was so traditional. I didn't know if she would be happy for me, give me advice, or scold me.

I didn't know if I had the energy to defend myself if my mom reacted harshly. But if she was on my side, if she was supportive and sympathetic, maybe I could deal with it. I needed someone whose shoulder I could cry on.

But I didn't know for a fact that my mom would be on my side. And that made everything so much more complicated.

I had no one I could talk to. I couldn't talk to my friends, and I couldn't turn to Ethan. I couldn't lean on anyone, ask advice, or cry about the situation I had gotten myself into.

I was completely alone, with no one to help me through this.

Charlie climbed onto the bed and curled into a ball on top of me. I ran my hands over him, relieved to have the warmth of another living body against me.

"I guess it's just you and me against the world again, huh, big boy?"

It was ironic that when I had moved to North Haven, I

had figured it was just me and my cat, starting over. I hadn't had anyone in my life: no friends, and I wasn't dating anyone. North Haven had been a clean slate.

And now? Now, I had Ethan in my life, a baby on the way, and friends pestering me to hang out.

And yet, after it all, I was still incredibly alone.

SEVENTEEN

ETHAN

She wouldn't talk to me.

I had that sinking feeling in my gut that I was losing her. It was just a matter of time before she was gone completely. No matter what I did, how I tried to get through to her, she wouldn't talk to me about what was bothering her. I had long stopped buying her act where she put on a cute little smile and told me that everything was "perfectly fine."

Three of my patients hadn't received their medication yet by the time I did my rounds, and I was highly strung.

"What do you think this is?" I snapped at Adriana, the first nurse I found after I'd been marching up and down the hallways, looking for someone to shout at. "It's like you think you don't have a job to do. What do you think you're getting paid for around here?"

She blinked at me. "Sorry, Dr. Cole."

"Sorry doesn't fix how you screwed up."

She shook her head, backing away from me until she was sure I wasn't going to say anything else before she turned and fled.

"What's wrong with you?" Nate asked, appearing behind me.

"I was almost an hour late for my rounds this morning, and despite having the extra time, the nurses didn't do anything they should have. It's like I have to do it all myself around here. Why the hell do we have nurses at all?"

"Wow. I'd love to meet whoever pissed in your coffee," he said sarcastically. "Why were you so late?"

I glared at him. It was Piper's off day, and I'd spent almost an hour on the phone with her, trying to figure out what the hell was going on with her. I wasn't going to tell Nate that, though. He didn't know anything about what was going on between me and Piper, and it was better that way.

"I had personal shit to take care of," I said flatly.

"You're never this worked up," Nate said. "Did you have a rough night with a patient?"

I shook my head.

"Lose someone?"

Not yet, I thought.

"No, it's not that," I said.

"Fine, you don't want to talk about it. Don't. I'm not going to beg you to tell me what's going on with you. But you know you can talk to me, right?"

"Yeah," I said and sighed. "Sorry. I'm just in a shitty mood."

"I didn't notice," Nate said with a chuckle. "I gotta go. I have paperwork to do."

I nodded and he walked away, hands in his pockets, whistling like he didn't have a care in the world. He was a damn good oncologist, but he looked like he should be on a beach somewhere.

How did someone like Nate saunter through life

without a care in the world? Why did losing patients not make him feel like a failure? Why were relationships so simple to him, and why was life so fucking easy for him?

I was pissed off, but I knew I wasn't being fair. We each had our cross to bear, wasn't that what everyone kept saying?

It sounded like bullshit to me. *Life* wasn't fair. So, whatever.

I turned to walk to the cafeteria. I would have liked something strong, like whiskey or vodka, but coffee would have to do when I had a workday ahead of me.

Adriana was in the cafeteria, too, heading toward a table with her lunch. When she saw me, she quickly looked away.

I knew what I had to do.

I walked up to her. She cringed when she saw me.

Dammit. I hated that my staff was afraid of me, but I couldn't blame them.

"Sorry about that back there," I said without fanfare. "It was unprofessional of me. I appreciate your hard work."

She seemed surprised, but she finally gave a quick nod. "Okay. Thanks."

I gave her a nod then quickly turned away to make my purchase at the counter. Then, I returned to my office, sipping the strong black coffee, getting irritated with myself for... well, being irritated.

What the hell was Piper doing to me? I was starting to put my job second when it came to her. When had I ever let anyone make me late for work? Not to mention the fact that I was so damn crabby, it was affecting everyone around me, including my patients.

And for what?

When everything had been perfect between us, it was okay. I had still been aware that I was allowing her to take up a space in my life I'd never let anyone occupy before. But it had been worth it because we'd been heading in a great direction.

Now, she was pulling away from me. She was distant, closed off. She wouldn't talk to me. When she told me everything was fine and that I didn't have to worry, I felt like it was me who was the problem. Why else would she not want to talk to me about it?

I racked my brain, trying to think of something I'd done wrong. But I always came up empty.

I looked at the paperwork that sat on my desk and scowled. God, I didn't feel like doing this at all.

I sat back in my chair and sighed. I liked the person I was when things had been great between me and Piper. When everything was fine. Now that things weren't okay, I was starting to slip back into the grumpy, sullen ass I'd been until now, and I hated this part of myself. I hated being so grim and closed off, so rude to everyone around me.

I had always expected the highest standards from the nurses and doctors that worked with me, but there was a difference between being strict and being rude. And sometimes, I knew, I crossed the line. It wasn't easy to work with me.

I'd always been aware of that.

The thing was, it had never bothered me before. I'd had a reputation. It was who I'd always been.

It was only now that things started changing for me, since Piper had come into my life almost four months ago. I realized with a pang that I didn't want to go back to a life without her where I was sullen and gruff and no one liked me.

Not even me.

I just had to find the key that would change things for us again.

Something had to be done.

The next morning, I got up earlier than usual, showered, and got ready. My mind was still filled with Piper and everything that went wrong between us, but I had other things to focus on today. The long-awaited performance review at the hospital was finally up, and I was to meet with the board in an hour.

When I arrived at the hospital, I waited outside the doors that led into the conference room in the administration area. I was nervous, my stomach tied in knots. If they liked what they heard today, there was a chance I could get a promotion. I had to put my best foot forward and not show my dark side that had returned the last couple of weeks.

When they called me in, I smiled at the five directors who sat in a row in front of me. I sat down at the table, cleared my throat, and looked at them expectantly.

"Good morning, Dr. Cole," one of them said.

"Good morning," I said.

"We've been looking at your files, and we're all impressed with your work. You're one of our top performing providers here."

I smiled. "That's always good to know."

"You're our top candidate for the position. We're very serious about who takes on the role of being a medical director. Your track record is excellent."

"Thank you," I said.

"We have a few questions we'd like to ask, though," another director—a woman—said.

I nodded. "Anything. I'm an open book."

"Right. Well, it's clear you're dedicated to your work. We feel it's important that you can keep your focus on your patients."

I nodded. "I'm willing to give whatever it takes, put in the extra hours. It's about the lives we save around here."

They nodded. They couldn't come out and ask about my home life, but I knew the fact that I was unmarried and without children probably worked in my favor.

"How would you feel about traveling and speaking at seminars?"

"I'm happy to share my knowledge and expertise," I said. "It would be an honor."

They nodded again.

"And how's your relationship with the staff?"

I stilled. How did they know about me and Piper?

"I'm not sure I understand the question," I said carefully.

"You have a reputation around here for being quite harsh toward them. It's said in some circles that you're unforgiving."

I realized they weren't talking about a romantic relationship. They were referring to the general way I treated the staff.

I nodded. "I'm aware that my approach to leadership can come off as gruff at times, but I demand excellence from my staff because of the gravity of our work. We're dealing with life and death in the ER, and one slip-up can be deadly. The staff is capable of extraordinary things. They wouldn't be here at this hospital if they weren't. I set high standards and expect the staff to meet them. Our patients deserve no less."

The directors glanced at each other and nodded.

They asked me a few more questions, and the interview stretched on until, finally, the chairman cleared his throat.

"Thank you, Dr. Cole. We'll let you know what our verdict is."

"Thank you for your time," I answered.

I stood, pushed my chair in, and left the conference room. Once I was around the corner and out of sight, I sagged against the wall and tried to take a deep breath. I'd panicked when I'd thought they were asking about Piper.

Why was I panicking? I wanted to be with her, and I'd wanted to go to HR a few times to tell them. She'd been the one to insist that we wait.

Well, there was no reason to wait any more. I'd just had my final interview. No matter if I got the job or not, we could finally go public with our relationship.

If it could still be called that.

It was time Piper and I had a chat about where this was headed. Was there still a relationship to declare at all? She hadn't given me any indication that she wanted to end things between us. But with her distance, it was impossible to imagine that she would want to keep going the way we were now.

When I reached my office, I sat down in the leather armchair and tilted my head back, eyes closed. This should have been a positive day for me. The interview had gone well, and everything was as it should be. There was a good chance I'd get the position.

But instead of wanting to celebrate, I felt miserable.

And it was all because of Piper. Since when did a woman get me down in the dumps like this?

Since I'd fallen for her.

EIGHTEEN

PIPER

The ringing tone was loud in my ear. My heart beat in my throat. I took a deep breath and let it out slowly, waiting for my mother to answer the phone.

I couldn't keep this a secret anymore.

"Hello?" my mom asked. "Honey, is that you?"

"Yeah, it's me, Mom," I said with a smile.

"Oh, it's so good to hear your voice," my mom said, and I could hear the smile in her voice as well. A pang of nostalgia and homesickness shot through me, and I squeezed my eyes shut.

"I'm sorry it's been a couple weeks since I last called. It's been incredibly busy at the hospital."

"Oh, sweetheart, you don't have to explain that to me. I know what your life is like. How are you doing?"

I swallowed hard. How was I doing? Terribly, if I had to be honest. The morning sickness was difficult to deal with and not only in the mornings, either. I felt the urge to throw up all the time, and often did, at any time during the day.

I had several new food aversions as well, and I felt

uncomfortable and bloated, even though I wasn't very far along at all.

And that was just the physical side of things. Emotionally, I was exhausted, stressed out, and panicked.

"I'm okay," I said.

"Are you still liking your job? Have you gotten settled in?"

I nodded. Over the past couple of months, I had been giving my parents updates about my life in North Haven, but I hadn't found the time to have long conversations with them.

"I have a couple of good friends," I said. "And I get along with my colleagues very well. It's a good place to work."

"And you're still liking North Haven?" she asked. "It's such a cute little town. I like the pictures you've sent."

"Yeah, it's great. People are really friendly here."

"Your dad and I will have to come visit soon," she said.

"How are things at home?" I asked, stalling for time.

"Oh, you know, quiet as usual. Your dad has started looking at online videos about woodwork, although we all know it's never going to happen." She laughed.

I could hear my dad shouting something in the background about how he was just preparing himself for greatness before he got started.

I chuckled. I missed my parents so much. Moving to North Haven had been a great idea and a wonderful move for my career. And it could have been the start of a great relationship, too.

The lump in my throat grew. Well, maybe it was better not to think about *that* too much.

"What's wrong, honey?" Mom asked.

"What do you mean?" I asked, lying back on my bed.

"I can hear something is bothering you. What's going on?"

My eyes welled up with tears. My mom had always been able to read me like a book.

I bit my lip. "Promise you won't be mad?" I asked.

"Sweetheart, it doesn't matter what you are struggling with. You'll always be my only daughter, and I'll always love you."

It wasn't a promise, but it was close enough.

I took a deep breath. "I'm pregnant."

My mom's stunned silence was exactly what I had expected.

She was disappointed in me, I was sure. Tears rolled over my cheeks.

"It wasn't just a one-night thing," I continued when my mom didn't say anything. "We're in a relationship. But he doesn't know about the baby, and I don't think he wants children. It wasn't exactly planned."

"No," my mom said softly, finally speaking. "I imagine it wasn't."

I hesitated.

"Honey, what are you going to do?" she asked.

"I might have to raise it without him," I said, choking on the words. "I don't want to force him to be in a relationship if he doesn't want to be a dad to this baby. But it might be hard for me without any help. I was thinking... I was hoping I could come back home if I need to."

"Hoping?" Mom asked, sounding incredulous. "Piper, what makes you think that it wouldn't be an option? You know our home is always open for you. You know we're never going to turn you away."

A sob racked my chest. I had been terrified of telling my

mom what was going on in my life. But she was being so nice about it, so understanding and kind.

"I really expected you to be mad," I said. "It's kind of a big deal."

"It is, but I've seen how you deal with everything else that happens in your life. You're strong, sweetie. You're going to get through this, and we'll be here to help you every step of the way."

"You have no idea how much that means to me," I said softly.

We talked for a short while longer. My mom asked about Ethan, about our relationship, and after I explained to her what it had been like, she was sympathetic.

"I do think you need to tell him the truth," she said. "But if he won't have a part of it, then we'll make the best of it together."

I agreed, happy that I had a place to go if I needed. When we ended the call, I felt so much better.

I set my phone down with a sigh and looked at Charlie, who was bathing himself at the foot of the bed.

"What do you think, big guy?" I asked him. "You think we should go back home?"

He ignored me, closing his eyes and curling himself up on the bed.

I took a deep breath and let it out slowly. One thing I knew about myself was that I could get through anything. I'd managed to break away from Chris and start over. I'd left home. I'd started a life away from everything I knew.

I could figure this out, too. It just felt awful now, as if there was no light at the end of the tunnel.

But I was a lot like Charlie, I decided.

I always landed on my feet.

Stretching out on the bed, I cuddled up against his soft, warm body. He was familiar, comforting.

Maybe moving home would be for the best. I missed my family.

I could return to Roanoke, where I belonged. It wasn't that I *didn't* belong in North Haven, but now that Ethan was so distant from me, I felt different about the town.

My heart already hurt from losing a little of the closeness Ethan and I had shared. If I lost him totally, the pain would be unbearable.

Which would make staying in North Haven impossible.

Even if I had to leave friends like Adriana and Jeremy behind.

Ethan and I were caught in a vicious cycle. The more time passed, the more he seemed to pull away. I knew that it was my fault because I'd been the first to pull back, but I couldn't help it.

I had a baby growing inside me. I was freaked out.

And I was terrified of telling Ethan that I was pregnant. He was so grumpy again lately, difficult to be around. He snapped at everyone at work, and when I tried to speak to him, it was like there was something blocking us off from each other, an invisible barrier.

It didn't matter how hard it was to tell him, though. He had a right to know.

I couldn't keep this away from him forever. But I didn't know *how* to tell him, and I didn't know what to expect.

We hadn't seen each other in a couple of days, to boot. I'd had two days off, and he'd been incredibly busy between work, with his review, and helping Viola with a couple minor emergencies.

Where there had been affection and warmth between us before, a cold chasm had sprung up between us.

I sat up on my bed, feeling sick. Was I going to throw up again?

Possibly.

I had to tell him. No more delays.

And then, after that, I could go home.

My stomach turned violently. I jumped off the bed, running to the bathroom. I fell to my knees in front of the toilet for the umpteenth time that day.

The way my life had fallen apart so quickly, it only seemed fitting.

NINETEEN

ETHAN

"Good morning, Dr. Green," I said, walking into one of the ICU rooms on my rounds for the day. "How are we feeling?"

"Fine," Dr. Green said solemnly. "Being on the other side of the clipboard is a whole different ballgame."

I nodded. "It's hard to be a passenger when you're used to being in the driver's seat."

Dr. Green was a pediatrician, and I knew all too well that medical professionals struggled when they were the patients.

"Let's get you healthy and out of here as soon as possible," I added when he only snorted at me. I walked to the cabinet and took out some supplies, ready to administer medication that the nurses weren't qualified to give him.

I prepared the syringe, chatting about the weather, trying to be polite and kind. I thought about Piper and the way she could get anyone to open up. I was willing to bet she could get someone like Dr. Green to smile and laugh rather than sit there on the bed sulking about the fact that he was the patient.

When I walked to Dr. Green, I took his arm and tapped him in the crook of his elbow, ready to find a vein. I sanitized the area with an alcohol swab.

Just before I pricked him with the needle, I froze. I looked at the syringe in my hand. It was the wrong medication. The pharmacy had sent the wrong med, and I had almost delivered it without checking first.

I swallowed hard.

"There seems to be a problem," I said softly. "I'll get a fresh vial for you."

"What's the problem?" Dr. Green asked, immediately curious.

I shook my head. "Just an issue with this vial. Nothing you need to worry about."

I pushed the nurse's button next to Dr. Green's bed and waited for a nurse to arrive. I was glad when it wasn't Piper.

"Please get another vial of this from the pharmacy," I said, writing a fresh prescription and handing it to the nurse who hurried away.

"Better safe than sorry," I said to the patient, smiling at him.

Although I was putting on a smile, I was reeling.

I had nearly given him medication that would have caused a serious problem, clashing with the meds he was already taking. I hadn't been paying attention. My mind had been on Piper.

I had caught my mistake before anything had gone wrong, but that didn't mean I was off the hook. Maybe I wouldn't be questioned over my mistake. No one would know what I had almost done.

But I knew.

And it was unacceptable. I couldn't afford to have something like this happen. Silly mistakes that hurt the patients were inexcusable. And all because I was worrying about Piper, thinking about her and what might happen between us.

When the nurse returned with the vial, I turned to the drawer and discreetly replaced it with the right medication. When I administered it, I continued chatting as if nothing had been wrong at all.

"Well, this should do the trick," I said, rubbing Dr. Green's arm after giving him his medication. "By tomorrow, we should have some good news. Hopefully, you'll be released before the weekend."

"Let's hope so."

His gruff attitude reminded me of my own, and I wondered if people saw me as such a pain in the ass all the time. The nurses complained about my attitude, but I always replied that we had people's lives in our hands.

This incident only proved my point. But it also reminded me that I wasn't perfect, either.

A small mistake because I was scatterbrained could have cost Dr. Green his life.

When I stepped out of the room, I looked around, making sure the halls were empty before I leaned against the wall and let out a shaky breath.

This shouldn't be happening. I was too stressed, too worried about Piper. It had me twisted in knots, and I was fucking up.

When I walked to my office, my cell phone rang.

It was Jared, my youngest brother. I decided to take the call. I was done with my rounds, and I could use a quick break.

"Well, if it isn't my little brother, the baseball star," I said. "Your call is the perfect distraction."

"Rough day?" Jared asked.

"You have no idea."

"Well, this might lift your spirits. You'll never guess who I hooked up with last night."

I chuckled, relieved to be thinking about something less serious. "You're right, I probably won't be able to."

"Daniela Rivera."

I blinked, trying to remember if that name should have been familiar.

"Oh, come on, Ethan," Jared said, sounding disgusted. "Don't tell me you don't know who she is."

"I can't place her," I admitted.

"The supermodel? She was a Victoria's Secret Angel last year. With the black feathers."

"Ah," I said, not really able to picture her, but Jared was satisfied. "Lucky you."

Jared chuckled. "Lucky? I hit the jackpot. She's incredibly hot. Plus, she has a lot of contacts, so the stream of supermodels will be never-ending from here on out."

I laughed. "You're really living the high life, aren't you?"

"You bet."

I smiled, listening to Jared rattle on about his escapades, the people he met, and the women he slept with. He often called me to brag about them. I think it was because I was willing to humor him. He was famous, young, and the world was at his feet.

It was good for him to have fun as long as no one got hurt. He'd been through hell like all us Cole brothers.

Part of me wondered why *I* wasn't having more fun. Sure, I had been responsible for a long time while my brothers had grown up, but even Jared, the youngest, was living it up in Boston now, completely independent. I had to start having fun, too. It was time I started relaxing and kicking back. It was time I stopped worrying about everything.

Maybe I had to get back in the game. Being involved in a committed relationship was complicated, and the whole idea of love scared me. Not that I would admit that to anyone.

But I knew I didn't want that. I only had eyes for Piper. Since I had met her, I hadn't wanted anyone else.

"So, what have you been up to?" Jared asked after finishing his update.

"Just work," I said. I didn't want to tell him about Piper at all. Maybe soon there wouldn't be anything to tell.

"You know what they say about all work and no play," Jared said with a chuckle.

"And you're a good example that the opposite is true, too."

Jared chuckled, willing to accept the subtle reproach.

"Make sure you get out and have some fun, bro," Jared said before we hung up.

"I will," I said half-heartedly.

When I ended the call, I dropped my head into my hands, elbows on my desk.

What was I supposed to do? I wouldn't be able to let Piper go without feeling a gaping hole in my life. She had changed me.

But I couldn't continue like this, either.

I picked myself up and focused on my paperwork. I couldn't continue moping over Piper. I would have to decide what to do about our relationship, but for now, work had to come first. I had to stay focused. I had to keep my head in the game. I couldn't allow mistakes like this morning to happen again.

But all this tension with Piper was about to come to a head. I could feel it.

TWENTY

PIPER

I was headed home after a long shift, and I was dead.

Lately, being on my feet the whole day was a challenge. It had never been difficult before, but I was more and more exhausted now, and getting sick every so often didn't make things better. At least I hadn't felt sick for the last couple of hours. I had taken to chewing pieces of ginger whenever I had a chance. It helped with the nausea.

I was walking toward the main entrance of the hospital, my eyes focused on the sliding doors, when suddenly, someone appeared in front of me. I'd nearly run into him before I realized it was Ethan.

My stomach twisted, and my heart did a little flip.

I still got butterflies when I saw him, but now it came with a pang of nerves.

"Piper," he said, his voice stern.

"Ethan," I answered, not sure what to expect.

If I'd been more alert, I might have avoided him in the hallway and tried to escape before he saw me. That was pathetic, I knew, but it was all I could manage lately. I had taken to avoiding him in the hallways and switching with other nurses if I ended up on his rounds because I didn't know what to say to him.

The word *coward* had come to mind more than once.

"Will you come over tonight?" he asked.

I looked around, surprised that he was standing in the middle of the hospital, asking me out as if we didn't have anything to hide.

"Tonight?" I asked in a small voice.

Ethan nodded. "I'd like to talk to you."

"Okay," I said softly.

Ethan nodded curtly before he turned around and walked away.

Oh, God. How was I going to do this?

I wanted to see him. I'd always wanted to see him. I got butterflies whenever I thought about any part of our relationship. I had never felt about anyone the way I felt about him.

But at the same time, I was terrified of how he would react when he found out that I was carrying his child when I knew he didn't want any children at all.

But it didn't matter. I had to tell him.

And maybe being alone with Ethan would help straighten out my mind and heart.

I went home to make sure Charlie had food, and I tried to calm down a bit. But it was no use. By the time I drove to Ethan's house, I was a nervous wreck.

When I knocked on the front door, he opened almost immediately, as if he had been waiting for me to arrive.

He stepped aside and let me in. He offered me something to drink—I only took water—and finally, we were settled on the couch in the living room. It was so formal and strained where usually we were very comfortable around each other.

"How was your performance review?" I asked.

"Fine," he said. "I'll hear their decision about the promotion soon."

"That's good," I offered. "I hope you get it."

He nodded, and we fell into silence. He had poured himself a glass of water, too, but it sat on the coffee table, untouched.

This couldn't be more awkward, I thought. *Where's the old Ethan? Where's his warmth?*

"You've been avoiding me," Ethan said bluntly.

"I haven't," I argued stubbornly, even though it was true. I should have just admitted to it. I was going to tell him what was going on, after all.

"I'm not an idiot, Piper. I know what it looks like when someone doesn't want to see me."

I blinked at him, not knowing what else to say.

"So, do you want to tell me what's going on?"

"Yes, I do need to talk to you," I started. "I have something to tell you."

I took a deep breath. It was now or never. But before I could continue, he interrupted me.

"You can't do this to me, Piper," he said angrily, his voice rising. "This is total bullshit, and you know it."

I looked at him with my mouth open. That old angry voice he used with the nurses was returning, and it made me recoil. And he hadn't even let me speak.

"What am I doing?" I asked.

He glanced at me. "I thought we were good. I thought we were going in the right direction. But now you're just pulling away from me. It's not right, and it needs to change."

"You're talking to me like you do at the hospital," I said, my heart pounding. "I don't like it, Ethan."

"You don't like how I act at the hospital?" he asked, his eyes narrowing.

"No, I don't. It would just be nice if you could be civil toward the staff, at least once. Or even me. So that I could feel like I'm not just a waste of your time."

Ethan shook his head. "You know how things are at the hospital. You can't tell me it's wrong. And you don't know what it's like for me at work. I have so much responsibility on me, and it's not too much to ask for the staff to be on the ball."

I was amazed. I didn't recognize the man sitting in front of me anymore. Was he really justifying his bad attitude at work and now here with me?

"So that makes it okay for you to yell at everyone? I heard how you treated Adriana the other day. You can't just bite everyone's head off all the time."

"If you can't accept who I am in the workplace, we need to seriously revise what's going on here," Ethan said angrily.

The words sunk like lead in the room.

I shook my head. It was better if I didn't tell him about the baby. I didn't want to continue the conflict with him, and telling him I was pregnant was liable to make him lose his temper completely.

It was clear he didn't want this relationship any longer. And I wasn't going to stick around to beg him. Sadness filled my core as I realized what I had to do.

"Yes, apparently we should," I said. "I don't think this is working."

Ethan frowned slightly. "What do you mean it's not working?"

I drew a breath. "It's just like you said. We need to revise."

We looked at each other. I felt frozen for a second as a

voice in my head called me a coward and begged me not to do this.

But another part inside me told that voice to be quiet.

"I'm sorry, Ethan," I said, looking down at my hands. "I don't think we should see each other anymore."

"Are you fucking kidding me?" Ethan asked, rising to his feet suddenly and staring at me in shock. "You're just going to end it?"

"This is something I've learned from experience," I said, feeling tears rush to my eyes. My stomach twisted as I spoke.

His eyes searched mine as I paused.

"If you're not happy, walk away," I said, my voice cracking.

I could hear the words, but it was as if I weren't speaking them myself. How was this happening? It felt all wrong, like a train wreck, but I didn't know how to stop it.

He bristled, and for a moment, I expected him to explode. Instead, he withdrew. He sank back down onto the couch and looked away.

"I think I need to go," I said when he didn't speak for a while. I wiped the tears from my eyes.

"You might want to take your things with you," he said flatly.

I wanted him to tell me to stay, that this was all wrong. His words were like a knife in my chest. This seemed so painless for him.

I stared at him. The longer the silence stretched out, the more a fiery anger took over the sadness in my chest.

I had a few outfits at his house, a hairbrush, a phone charger. I would have to come back for those if I didn't take them now. I was shocked at how easy it was for him to tell me to get them.

"Fine," I said and stormed deeper into his house. My eyes welled with tears again as I moved from his bedroom to his bathroom, getting my things together. My vision blurred, and I blindly loaded everything into my arms. When I hurried back to the front door, Ethan was still sitting on the couch. He didn't do anything. He didn't even get up to let me out the door.

Instead, I closed the door behind me and walked to my car, alone.

When I drove home, I fell apart. I parked the car and then dragged myself inside the house to sob in bed.

Maybe it won't hurt this bad forever. Maybe it's for the best.

I hadn't walked away from Chris when I should have, and it had turned out badly for me for a long time. Calling it quits now was better. This way, I could protect myself.

Despite trying to convince myself that I had done the right thing, I felt my heart shatter into a million pieces. Leaving Ethan was the hardest thing I had ever done and driving away from him felt like I was leaving the most important part of myself behind.

TWENTY-ONE

PIPER

When I had broken up with Chris so many times, it had never been shattering, because at the back of my mind, I had always known that we would get back together again. It had been an emotional rollercoaster with Chris, up and down all the time, because a breakup was still a breakup. But it wasn't necessary to mourn a relationship that would start up in a couple of days again.

With Ethan, it was different. The pain was almost unbearable.

It was a different kind of grief, though. It was something I felt I had done myself. I was to blame for the pain I felt because I had chosen to end things with Ethan.

The truth was, I hadn't been ready. I hadn't thought about it.

Sure, I had thought about what it would mean to lose him, but I had never considered that I would be the one to push him away.

Now that it was this far, I couldn't imagine how I was going to get through it.

It took me two days of trying to survive before I decided

that I had to do something. I couldn't just move on. I couldn't leave him behind and forget everything that we'd shared.

I had to tell him about the baby, at least. If nothing else. Even if it meant that we would never be together again, he had the right to know.

And maybe, if I told him what was going on, he would understand why I had pushed him away. Maybe he would forgive me.

I wasn't sure if I wanted him to take me back, but knowing that he was upset with me was gut-wrenching.

I waited for him outside his office before my rounds, hoping that his schedule hadn't changed.

I kept glancing at the time, nervous about seeing him.

Finally, I saw him coming toward me down the corridor.

"Can I help you, Nurse Edwards?"

I cringed when he called me that, so formal and distant.

"Can we talk?" I asked.

"Is it about a patient?" he asked, unlocking his office.

"No."

"Is it about anything work-related?" he asked.

"You know it's not," I said.

"In that case, we have nothing to say to each other," he said and stepped into his office, closing the door in my face.

Shit.

I went through my rounds, doing my chores, getting through the day one horrible step at a time.

As if my emotional state affected my pregnancy, I threw up even more than usual. To the point where Adriana asked me if I was sick.

"I just think it's a stomach bug," I lied. "I'll take something for it."

"I'm worried about you," she said. "You're so distant lately. And you look so sad all the time."

I pulled up my shoulders. "You know what it's like to be a nurse. Sometimes, it just gets to you."

She narrowed her eyes at me. "I don't think you're telling me what's going on," she said. "We have a tough job, but I love it. Everyone here does. And you did until recently, too. I don't think the work is taking a toll on you. I think it's something else."

I was getting irritated with her pushing for an answer, although I knew she was just concerned about me. But I was upset that Ethan wouldn't even speak to me, not here at the hospital or anywhere else. And I didn't know what else to do.

"Well, when you figure out what's bugging me, will you let me know, too?" I snapped.

I cringed, immediately regretting my words as a pang of guilt shot through me.

It was unfair of me to be rude to Adriana. She was being a good friend.

"I'm sorry, Adriana," I said. "That was a shitty thing to say."

She told me it was okay, and we split up to continue with our work.

But it felt like my life was falling apart, and I was struggling to keep it together.

As I continued my tasks for the day, I started considering what it would mean to go back home. I had to quit my job here. I couldn't keep running into Ethan. Seeing him again was terrible. It felt like it ripped my heart out of my chest all over again. Running into him every day was going to be awful.

Not to mention the fact that he refused to talk to me.

He was set on keeping it strictly business between us, and I couldn't do that.

It was time to go back home to Roanoke. It was time to accept defeat, to move back to my family and have my baby where I would have love and support.

After work, Adriana found me.

"Let's go out for a drink," she said. "It looks like you need it."

I sighed. "Why don't you come over to my place instead? We'll have pasta and watch a movie."

Ariana frowned. "Why don't you want to go out?"

"Because I'm pregnant," I blurted out.

There. I finally said it.

I hadn't expected to let it slip, but it felt good.

Adriana's eyes widened. "Oh, my God," she said.

I nodded. "I know. It's a long story. I'll tell you all about it. And then I'll have to explain to you why I need to leave, why I need to go back home."

Adriana winced. "Let's go and talk, first. Let's see how necessary it is for you to leave."

At my place, on the couch with two sodas and Charlie curled up on my lap, I told her everything. About the one-night stand that turned out to be the infamous Dr. Cole, our secret relationship, and how I'd gotten pregnant. How he'd said he didn't want children and the downward spiral from there. When I was done talking, my cheeks wet with tears, Adriana shook her head. She reached over to scratch Charlie between the ears before she talked.

"You deserve better than Ethan," she said.

I looked up at her. "This isn't his fault, it's mine."

"I know. But you're not the only one in this relationship. It always takes two to tango."

I nodded. I knew I'd screwed up, but it was nice to

know that my friend was supportive. And it was even better to know that she finally knew the whole story and that there were no secrets between us.

"I have to leave North Haven," I said. "I can't raise this baby all on my own. And I can't live in this small town seeing Ethan everywhere."

"I hate this, but I understand why you want to leave," she said.

"I don't know what to do with his things. I can't see him again, it's too painful."

Adriana looked at her wristwatch. "Why don't we put it all in a box right now and leave it on his doorstep?"

"What?"

"That way, you don't have to face him. He's still at the hospital. He's on night shift tonight."

I hadn't realized that, but I knew Adriana was right. And she was being such a good friend.

"Okay," I said.

Together, we moved through my house, packing up everything that belonged to Ethan. When we drove to his place together, I broke down in tears. Adriana talked me through the whole thing, being supportive, kind, and encouraging.

We walked to his doorstep together and put the box in front of the front door.

"This is good," Adriana said. "The end of a chapter."

I nodded. She was right, it was the end of a chapter.

And it was the right thing to do.

But if it was the right thing to do, why did it hurt so damn bad?

TWENTY-TWO

ETHAN

The night at the ER was grueling. We'd had three emergency cases come in, all of which had been touch and go at one point or another. By the time I was finally able to breathe again, I had been on my feet for over twelve hours. I was running on fumes.

The upside of being so busy at the hospital was that I hadn't had a chance to think about Piper and where things had gone between us.

I had never been in a relationship as serious as I had been with Piper and losing her hurt like hell.

Now that I sat in my car, driving home, the sun rose above the horizon. I was bombarded by images of Piper, the sound of her laughter, the happiness I had felt when we had been together.

Then, I saw the expression on her face when she broke up with me, and the sheer horror I had felt when I lost her came flooding back.

I tried to shove the thoughts away, not wanting to think about it at all. But no matter what I did, I couldn't stop thinking about her.

"Dammit, if she doesn't want me, why should I care?" I asked myself out loud.

Because I was in love with her, I realized. That was why I cared.

And it didn't matter now. Because I'd lost her.

I started thinking about other things, trying to focus on work. I had dealt with grief before. Getting through my parents' death had been difficult but not impossible.

I'd have to take it day by day.

But this was a very different kind of loss, and I was completely unequipped to handle it.

I pulled into my driveway and parked. I climbed out of my car and walked to the front door, not looking forward to my time off.

I froze when I saw a box of my things on the porch.

It was everything I had left at her house. She had brought it while I was gone so that she wouldn't have to talk to me again.

The sight hit me hard. I almost staggered back, gasping for breath.

This was really it, wasn't it? Piper and I were over.

I picked up the box and carried it into the house. I closed the door behind me and stood in the middle of my living room, trying to decide what I was going to do. Where was I supposed to put these things? I was never going to be able to look at any of these items again without thinking of her, of what we'd had.

I slammed the box to the floor.

Everything in it fell out—my clothes, my toiletries, and a framed picture of the two of us. I'd taken it to her house so she could have me close to her whenever I wasn't there.

The glass had cracked down the middle of the photograph, splitting the two of us. I sat down on the closest couch, putting the broken picture on the coffee table.

I scrubbed my face with my hands.

"This is for the best," I told myself. "This is how it's supposed to be."

I wasn't sure I would believe myself, but if I tried to say it over and over again, maybe eventually I would get there.

I had to focus on my career, anyway. I'd become too dependent on Piper, and it was dangerous to be too dependent on anyone. I had to stay strong, a lone wolf. I had to be the king of my castle, and the only way I could make sure that nothing went wrong was if this castle was a fortress.

She'd wanted to talk to me at the hospital. She'd tried once or twice, and a couple of times she had looked in my direction, probably hoping that I would talk to her.

But it was too late. I have tried so many times before, and she'd avoided me. Now, what could she possibly have to say that would make anything better?

Besides, talking to her would have hurt too much. It was why, after breaking up, I hadn't wanted her to say anything that wasn't work-related. I had to stay strong. I had to keep my distance.

Even though all I wanted was Piper in my arms.

"Dammit!" I shouted into my empty house.

I stood up, collected the stuff on the floor that fell out of the box and carried it to my bedroom. I threw it into the back of my closet and closed the closet doors again. I stripped off all my clothes, walked to the bathroom, and turned on the cold water, not bothering with the hot.

When I stepped under the spray, the cold water stung like needles when it hit my skin. But the pain was welcome. It was better than the pain I felt after losing Piper. At least, when I was trying to survive under the water, I wasn't thinking about Piper and everything I'd lost when she'd walked out of my life.

I stood under the freezing spray until my skin was bright red. When I'd turned off the water and toweled off, I walked to my bedroom and sat in my towel.

She was everywhere in the room. I could smell her on the blankets I sat on. It felt weird not having her here.

And dammit, that made me miserable.

I wanted to talk to her. I wanted to know where it had gone wrong between us. But it wasn't just that. I wanted to tell her about my day, how we'd managed to save all three lives that could have been lost tonight. I wanted to share with her how hard it had been to pull them through and how good it had felt to save them after all.

And I wanted to listen to her tell me about her day as we cuddled in bed, her voice melodious and her skin soft.

Without her, my life was empty.

The next day was my day off, and I climbed into the car and headed to Owen and his fiancée, Ruby's place. When I pulled into the driveway, Maisy ran out to greet me with her auburn pigtails bouncing as she ran.

"Uncle Ethan!" she called.

"There's my girl," I said, swinging her into the air, grinning when she squealed in delight.

It was the first time I'd smiled in days.

Gavin and Jolie arrived just after I did. We three brothers retreated to the kitchen to grab a couple of beers together while Ruby and Jolie played with Maisy.

"Maisy's entering a new stage of sassiness, the little

diva," Owen complained. "Ruby's better at handling her than I am."

Ruby wasn't Maisy's mother, but since Ruby and Owen had become an item, Ruby had taken the role as if she'd always been meant to be there. Maisy looked up to her as a mother.

Owen and Gavin joked about a few things, but I didn't follow the conversation. Instead, I looked over at where Jolie and Ruby were playing with Maisy, and I realized how good things had been with Piper.

The past few weeks, I'd been blessed with what I'd lost all those years ago when my parents had died.

It suddenly hit me. She'd filled a gaping hole in my life. And it wasn't a hole that could be filled by just any woman. No, Piper was special.

And only now, I realized what I'd had.

But it was too late. She was gone.

I just hadn't been enough for her.

My mouth went dry, and I wiped a line of sweat from my forehead.

"What's up with you, Ethan?" Gavin asked, pulling me back to the conversation.

"I'm just tired after a rough week," I said.

Gavin frowned. He'd noticed Piper wasn't with me, I was sure. But he wasn't going to ask about it in front of Owen.

Later, I would have to tell him that we'd broken up. I wasn't looking forward to it, though, and not just because I didn't want to admit that I'd lost her.

I didn't want to admit that I was missing some big things in my life.

Love and family.

TWENTY-THREE

ETHAN

When I opened my eyes on my second day off in a row, I was alone in my bed.

I had one thought.

Fuck.

I couldn't carry on like this for the rest of my life. A life without Piper seemed like a black hole, empty and hopeless, and I didn't want to do this anymore. It had been hard to deal with while I had been at work, but at least I'd had a lot to distract me. But now that I had no distractions at all, I couldn't stop thinking about her, and the ache was unbearable.

I wanted her back. I wanted her in my life. I wanted to wake up with her for the rest of my life, and I never wanted to spend another day without her.

I wasn't going to let things end with her. Not without a fight.

I jumped out of bed and got dressed, skipping my usual coffee as I headed out to the car. I didn't want to waste another minute.

It took everything I had not to break all the traffic rules and race to the hospital.

When I parked, I jumped out of the car and ran into the hospital. I headed to the staff room where the nurses usually took breaks. When I burst in, not wearing my white coat, the nurses who were drinking coffee together looked up at me and frowned. They seemed unsure how to react to me now that I wasn't on duty.

Piper wasn't with them, and I left the staff room without saying anything.

I searched everywhere for her—the locker room, the nurses' station, the supply rooms, the cafeteria.

"Ethan," Nate said. I jumped. "What the hell are you doing?" He looked me up and down. "Are you okay?"

"Fine," I said. "I need to find Piper."

"Who?" Nate asked, but I didn't have time to explain to him what was going on.

I spotted the nurse with the black hair Piper always hung out with and ran to her.

"Adriana!" I called out.

She turned around and frowned when she saw me, clearly taking in that I wasn't wearing my doctor's coat.

"Where is she?" I asked.

"Who?"

I shook my head. "Come on, don't act dumb. Piper."

"I'm on duty," she said flatly and started turning away from me.

"Wait," I said, and she stopped, although she wasn't looking at me. "Just tell me where she is. I know you know about us. Please, Adriana."

"She doesn't want to talk to you," she said.

"I know." I nodded and took a deep breath, letting it out

slowly. "But I need to talk to her, even if she has nothing more to say to me."

Adriana blinked at me, opening her mouth and closing it again without saying anything. I probably looked like a madman with my eyes dilated and my hair wild.

"I can't let her slip away," I pleaded.

"I can't believe this," she said.

"What?"

She let out a breath, and I couldn't understand her expression.

"She's on her way to HR."

"What?" I asked. "Why?"

"She's handing in her two-weeks' notice."

"What?" I cried out. "She can't leave!"

Adriana drew her mouth into a line.

"Why the hell would she want to leave? Surely, it couldn't be because of what happened between us?"

Adriana stared at me.

God, I had to stop her.

I couldn't wait for her answer. I turned and ran down the hallway, headed toward the administration offices.

Suddenly, the hospital seemed bigger than ever before. I turned down the long corridors, trying to avoid running into people as my shoes squeaked on the floors.

It was ironic how many times I'd wanted to go to HR to talk to them about me and Piper, to announce our relationship so that we could do it right. She'd been the one to ask me to wait so that I could have my meeting with the review board. She'd been the one to make sacrifices to allow me to stay comfortable.

She'd done so much in our relationship.

What had started out as a steamy night of sex had

ended up being the most special time I'd had with a woman. I couldn't let her slip through my fingers.

I hoped that she would hear me out. I hoped that she would give me a chance to talk to her, to tell her how I felt. Maybe it was a little later than it should have been. I should have confessed to her earlier what I felt for her. But I'd been too damn scared of getting hurt.

And even though I hadn't wanted to admit what I felt to her, there was no denying it.

I loved her.

I needed her. And if she left...

God, I hoped I wasn't too late.

When I finally rounded the last corner, I saw Piper. She sat on a chair outside the doors, her hands clasped together. I skidded to a stop and nearly lost my balance.

She looked up at me. Her eyes were a little sunken with dark circles beneath them, and her skin was a little sallow. She looked like she hadn't slept at all. She looked as if she felt as terrible as I did.

Though my heart went out to her that she looked so down, seeing her like that gave me hope. There was a chance, even if it was the smallest chance, that she might be struggling without me as much as I was struggling without her.

"Ethan?" she asked, looking confused. She stood carefully, as if holding herself up was hard work. She turned to face me, shoulders squared, her arms folded over her chest. "What are you doing here?"

This moment was my one chance to make her understand. I had to do it just right.

I couldn't lose her.

TWENTY-FOUR

PIPER

The last thing I'd expected was for Ethan to show up, running around the corner and nearly crashing into the wall, as I waited to speak to the head of human resources.

He was out of breath, his cheeks flushed. His eyes were wild. I'd never seen him like this, so flustered and vulnerable.

"Don't go in there," he said in a breathy voice. "Piper, please."

I shook my head. "Ethan, I can't do this. I can't stay here in North Haven anymore if we're not going to be together."

"Just let me talk to you first. After you hear me out, if you still want to resign, then you can. But I've got to talk to you first."

"I have an appointment," I started, but he looked so serious. He was seriously upset.

"Okay," I finally said.

The door opened and a woman appeared. "Ms. Edwards?"

I bit my lip. "Could I just have a moment before we start?" I asked her.

The woman glanced at Ethan and then at me before she nodded and returned to her office. "All right."

I looked at Ethan, butterflies in my stomach.

"Can we go sit outside?" he asked. "The garden out there is always quiet."

I sighed. "Ethan, I don't have time."

But something in his eyes made me back down. He had something important to say, and I knew I'd rather not hear it in the cold, sterile hallway.

"Okay, lead the way."

We walked through the hospital in awkward silence. It was weird seeing Ethan at work without his doctor's coat on, ignoring all the doctors and nurses passing. He was here just as himself—not as a doctor, not as my boss, not as anything else.

We walked through a door I hadn't ever seen before, and Ethan led me to a small garden that was beautifully decorated with large trees, a water feature, and benches that faced it. The entire area was empty of people, leaving Ethan and me to talk in peace.

Ethan gestured toward a bench, and I walked to it and sat down. He sat next to me.

"Piper," he started, and he swallowed hard. He shifted on the bench, turning to the side so that he faced me, and I did the same.

He looked nervous. His brow was bright with sweat.

"What is it?" I asked.

He took a deep breath.

"I'm in love with you."

I blinked at him. "What?"

"From the moment I saw you walk into The Tavern that

day, I knew you were someone special," he started. "And ever since then, you're all I've wanted, all I've cared about. Did you know that, Piper? Did you know that I haven't been able to think about anyone or anything else since I first touched you? Since I felt how wonderful it was to be with you?"

I looked at him, not sure if he was expecting an answer. If he was, I couldn't respond if I tried. I was speechless.

"You're the best thing to ever happen to me. I'd be crazy to let you slip away. Don't leave. Stay. Give me another chance."

My cheeks burned. He was confessing his love to me. I couldn't believe what I was hearing.

I couldn't believe that he felt the same way I did. I'd thought he hadn't cared for me anymore when he'd started withdrawing from me like that.

"I know how difficult I can be." He stood up and ran a hand through his thick brown hair, pacing a bit. "Hell, I can be a real asshole sometimes. I know it. It's a defense mechanism. I thought that if I denied how I felt, it wouldn't hurt to lose you when it inevitably happened. I thought if I didn't put my feelings into words, I'd be safe. I was so fucking scared of losing someone again, ever since... ever since I lost my parents."

I nodded and reached toward him, squeezing his hand. He swallowed hard.

"But I did lose you, and it's hell, Piper. I've realized what you mean to me. I don't want to be without you. And I'm done with the wall I've built around myself. I'm ready to let all that go, I swear to you. Just say you'll stay."

He came back to sit beside me on the bench, staring into my eyes, waiting for my response.

My heart filled as I looked into his blue eyes. He was

saying everything I'd wanted to hear for so long. His words were an elixir, and I loved every moment of it.

And I knew that I felt the same. I loved him, too.

But it wasn't that simple. He might have held back from telling me his feelings because of the fear of losing me. But I was holding back for a different reason.

"Why aren't you saying anything?" Ethan asked. "If you don't want this..." He let his breath out in a shudder, his voice trailing off.

Would he just let me walk away if that was what I wanted?

"It's not that," I said. "It's not that at all."

"Then what is it?"

I suddenly felt lightheaded. Every time I'd tried to tell Ethan I was pregnant, it had blown up in my face.

The other times, I'd prepared myself for it, figuring out the words I was going to say.

Now, I'd been caught off guard. I hadn't rehearsed the right lines, and I suddenly found it difficult to speak.

If I told him now, after he'd confessed his feelings to me, what would happen? Would he change his mind when I told him the truth? Fear mounted in my belly. Maybe he'd take back everything he said after knowing I was carrying his child.

I took a deep breath.

It was time. No matter what the consequences were.

"I'm pregnant," I finally said.

Ethan frowned, stunned into silence.

"What?"

My eyes welled up with tears until they spilled onto my cheeks.

"I'm going to have a baby, Ethan."

He blinked at me, and I couldn't read his face. My pulse

quickened as I started to explain, the words tumbling out in a panic.

"I wanted to tell you, but every time I tried, something came up. And then you told me you didn't want kids. I was so terrified of losing you, so I didn't say anything. I know I was a coward, but I couldn't do it." I was sobbing by the time I managed to finish explaining.

"Oh, my God, Piper," he finally said, taking both my hands in his. "You should have told me."

"I tried," I cried. "But I was so scared. I couldn't bear the thought of losing you, Ethan."

He shifted closer to me, wrapping me in his arms. I buried my face in his neck, crying on his shoulder. I had been carrying so much stress and tension with me for two weeks. Finally, I was able to let it all out. I was free of the heavy weight that this secret had put on me.

"You're pregnant," he said.

But instead of the anger and resentment I expected to hear in his words, his voice was full of joy. I looked up to see him smiling.

"You sound happy," I said, surprised.

"I am." His eyes were soft, his voice gentle. "We're going to start a family, Piper."

"But you don't want children," I said, frowning.

"I want a life with you. Whatever that means. And if we're going to have a baby, I want that, too. I love you, Piper. Don't you understand?"

"I love you, too, Ethan," I whispered, more tears rolling down my cheeks.

He wanted me. He wanted the baby. I'd been so scared he would reject me because I didn't fit into his plans, but I was wrong.

He wanted *us*.

And that was the best thing he could ever say.

"We're going to figure it out, okay?" Ethan asked.

I nodded.

"If you still want to quit your job, you should do what you need to do. But you should know that I'm going to do everything in my power to make sure we're okay. I don't want a life that revolves around work. I thought it was enough, but it's not. I want a life with you. That's all that matters. I didn't understand it before I met you. But I do now."

He bent down, pressing his mouth against mine. I wrapped my arms around his neck, breathing in his intoxicating scent. I got lost in him as he kissed me.

"I love you," I whispered. "I don't want to leave North Haven. And I don't want to stop working here. I was just trying to find a way to cope with losing you. But now that you're back, everything is perfect."

"Then let's get out of here," Ethan said.

He led me to his car and took me back to his place. Walking in through the door with him felt like coming home. A real home. A home where I belonged and where I wanted to be forever.

Ethan led me through the house and to the bedroom. There, he lay me on the bed and kissed me. Slowly, he started undressing me, and every kiss he planted on my skin felt like it wiped away the pain, the hurt, and the tears. He kissed my cheeks, moving down to my chest, and he slowly moved to my stomach.

"I can't wait to start this new life with you," he whispered. "To start a family of our own."

I smiled down at him, happier than I'd ever been.

When Ethan moved even farther down, I opened my

legs. He closed his mouth over my sex, and I moaned and cried out.

He was gentle with me, soft and tender. I writhed on the bed as he ran his hands over my body, worshipping every inch of me. With his mouth on my folds, his tongue circling my clit, he made me gyrate in pleasure, building an orgasm at my core that was stronger than anything I'd experienced with him before.

When I fell apart, the climax took over as waves of pleasure washed over me. He was right there to catch me and put me back together again.

After I recovered from my orgasm, Ethan moved up my body, planting kisses as he went along. My skin was on fire, my nerve endings alive, and I moaned until he closed his mouth over mine, swallowing my cries. He slid his erection into me while he kissed me, his cock thick and hard, and it split me open.

I cried out and panted when I felt him slide home, filling me up.

I loved feeling his uncovered length inside me. It felt so much more personal, so much closer.

I trembled underneath him.

"You mean everything to me," he said and kissed me again.

His lips were still locked on mine when he started moving in and out of me. Slowly at first, and then faster and faster. My breathing changed, becoming shallow and erratic as he rode me harder and faster.

But this wasn't fucking.

It was making love.

I orgasmed a second time, crying out, the ecstasy again so much more powerful this time. I wasn't sure if it was because of our connection now that we were close again, the lack of condom, or the fact that I was pregnant that made everything so amazing with him.

Maybe it was a combination of all three.

Ethan rolled us over, holding onto me when he rolled onto his back, flipping me over so that I sat on top of him. I yelped and then giggled.

"You've never done that before," I said in a breathy voice.

"You're teaching me to take risks."

I laughed. "I don't think this is the same."

He chuckled and twitched his cock inside of me so that I moaned.

I started moving on top of him, sliding his cock in and out of me. As he drove deeper into me, our bodies became one. I didn't know where I ended and he began.

I rocked my hips harder back and forth, riding him with everything I had, and I felt him grow harder and thicker inside me.

When he orgasmed, I tightened around him, and he bit out a cry. I felt his cock pulsate, pumping his warm release against my insides, filling me up even more than he already was, and the sensation pushed me over the edge into one last climax.

I collapsed on his chest as my body took over, muscles contracting as I shivered with pleasure.

Finally, after we both calmed down, we lay like that for the longest time. I felt his heart beating against my cheek, and we breathed in unison, relearning each other, finding each other again.

And this time, never letting go.

We were going to do this together, he and I.

I had never met a man like Ethan before, and for the first time ever, I was truly in love, truly happy. He was his own person, and I was my own as well, but when we were together, we complemented each other so that we were perfect together.

When I rolled off him, Ethan pulled me tightly against his side and dropped a kiss in my hair. I knew that he wasn't ever going to let me go again.

And I wasn't going to find a reason to leave again, either.

This was where I wanted to be. Happy, in love, and in Ethan's arms.

TWENTY-FIVE

ETHAN

Piper's having a baby. We're going to be parents.

Just a few short weeks after we reunited, Piper was far enough along that we could find out the sex of the baby.

I sat with her in the waiting room, holding her hand. She squeezed my fingers tightly, bouncing one leg with nervous tension.

"It's going to be fine," I reassured her.

"Why are you so calm about this?" she asked. "This is your first time, too."

I laughed. "This is exciting, babe. And I know we're going to have a perfect, happy, healthy baby no matter what."

The truth was that I was shitting myself. I'd seen enough medical emergencies to know how much could go wrong in pregnancy. Every discomfort Piper had, every new symptom, sent me down a spiral of worry, though I tried not to show it.

But I knew that Piper and I were going to get through

this together. No matter what came our way, we were in this as a team.

And I was thrilled that I was going to be a father.

The one thing I knew for a fact was that we were not alone. I had a bunch of brothers who could help us out, and everyone was bursting with joy that we'd have a new addition soon.

"Ms. Edwards?" the nurse called, and Piper stood.

We followed the nurse to the technician's office where Piper changed into a gown and waited. Finally, a warm, middle-aged woman greeted us.

"Shall we see what's under the hood?" she asked.

Piper and I laughed at the way she said it. She applied jelly to Piper's skin and slid the wand around her belly, which was just starting to show a little bulge that week. On the screen, gray images appeared on a black background.

"Here you go," the tech said, and I saw the shape of a baby come into focus.

When I looked at Piper, her eyes were glued to the screen and welling up with tears.

Suddenly a fast, thudding sound filled the room.

"That's the heartbeat," the tech said.

I looked at Piper, and my heart melted. That was our baby we were hearing. This was what we had made, together.

"Okay, what do we have here?" the technician muttered, and she shifted the wand again and again, frowning at the screen. "Ah," she said. "Baby is playing along. Here we go. It's... a girl."

She looked at us with a broad grin.

Piper looked at me with wide eyes.

"Oh, my God," I gasped. "We're having a girl!"

The tech laughed and nodded. I grabbed Piper and hugged her tightly.

"Are you happy?" she asked me.

"Happier than any man could ever be," I said and kissed her.

The rest of the appointment wrapped up fast. Piper dressed and then we walked back through the waiting area where other couples were about to hear the good news about their bundles of joy, too.

When we climbed in the car, I drove Piper out of town.

"Where are we going?" she asked.

"You'll see," I said.

I drove into a forested area, up into the mountains, following a winding road that curled through nature. It was beautiful, with the air cooler at the higher elevation. When the road opened onto a clearing, we parked at an overlook point that allowed us to see all of North Haven below, nestled in the wilderness all around it.

"I've never seen it like this," Piper said. "It's so beautiful."

"It is," I said. "I wanted to show you the town from this spot so you could take it all in at once. Down there is where we're going to make a life that's better than anything either of us could ever have dreamed of."

She smiled. "I like that idea."

I took a deep breath as she gazed at the view.

I sank to one knee and reached for a small box in my back pocket.

When Piper noticed, she clasped her hand to her mouth.

"What are you doing?" she asked through her fingers.

"Piper, you've made me happier than I ever thought I could be," I said.

I opened the box and produced a glittering diamond ring that Jolie had helped me pick out. I'd bought it weeks ago and had been saving it for just the right time.

"Will you marry me, Piper? Will you be with me forever?"

She started crying. Through the tears, she nodded.

"Yes, Ethan."

I stood and kissed her, and she clung to me, holding me tightly for the longest time.

"Yes," she whispered again. "A thousand times, yes."

I kissed her again, slipping the ring onto her finger.

EPILOGUE

PIPER

Five Months Later

"I look like I'm about to pop," I said, looking in the mirror.

Jolie, my soon-to-be sister-in-law, laughed. "Don't be silly. You're beautiful."

The ivory dress accentuated my rather gigantic baby bump, but it fell to the floor in soft folds and it made me look like a princess. I couldn't deny it.

"I think it's great that you're getting married before the baby comes," Adriana said, standing on my other side in her lavender maid-of-honor dress.

"Me too," Jeremy said, tears in his eyes. He looked dapper in his tux and blond hair combed to the side. "Although I do think you're cutting it right down to the wire with the timing of everything," he added with a laugh.

"I still have ten days till my due date," I reminded him.

"Come on, Jeremy. You know Little Miss Perfectionist here had to get every tiny detail just perfect for the wedding," Adriana said. "She *needed* all those months of planning."

Ruby, my other future sister-in-law, adjusted my gown. "Well, I think you did a great job, Piper. It looks great out there."

"Yeah, and I love my purple princess dress!" Maisy exclaimed, twirling in her little flower girl gown. We all laughed.

I looked at my friends in the mirror and smiled. I was amazed at how quickly my life had changed.

Ethan and I were happier than we'd ever been. We were hopelessly in love with each other, and our relationship had grown deeper and stronger each day. I knew I was the luckiest woman alive.

I shuddered every time I remembered how close I'd come to losing him. But the memory just made me want to hang on even tighter to him.

Ethan had gotten the promotion to medical director. Ironically, the new position had helped Ethan to relax a bit at work. He was still committed to excellence, but his higher rank at the hospital had given him a new perspective and a greater appreciation for all the staff. There were no more orders barked at nurses and no more bad attitude.

Of course, I liked to think I had something to do with that, as well.

I loved that he'd completely become the man he was meant to be. He was even more incredible than the Ethan I'd met nearly a year ago. The rough exterior to keep himself safe was long gone.

I'd just begun my maternity leave. Charlie and I had moved in with Ethan after the proposal, and were happy in our new home. Ethan and I had converted an empty room into the nursery, and we'd decorated it to the nines in pale pink and sunny yellow.

Everything was perfect.

"It's time!" Adriana said, and we all hurried to our places.

Maisy was the first to walk down the aisle, tossing her flower petals and smiling her gap-tooth grin.

The ceremony was small and beautiful. Only close friends and family came. My parents had driven up from Roanoke, and there wasn't a single dry eye in the little chapel on the edge of town as my father and I walked down the aisle.

As I moved toward Ethan at the front of the chapel, he looked at me with such love that I nearly melted. The world fell away when we stared into each other's eyes.

This moment was my dream come true.

We exchanged vows, and we kissed our first kiss as husband and wife. Everyone cheered, and my heart soared. Even the baby was excited. She was kicking up a storm!

At the reception, everyone let loose and danced. I sat down to rest after two songs, unable to keep going.

Adriana sat down next to me, out of breath.

"This is hands down the best wedding I've ever been to," she said. "But I think it's because I'm so directly involved." She smiled at me, but she frowned when she saw my face. "What's wrong?"

I was holding my stomach. I'd started cramping earlier, but it had been nothing serious. I'd had minor, occasional contractions for a couple of days now. My obstetrician, Dr. Conrad, had said my body was getting ready for the big push and that real labor could still be days away.

I'd thought these contractions were the same, but they were getting stronger. *Much* stronger.

"I think something's wrong," I said, drawing in air sharply.

I cried out when another sharp pain spread across my stomach. Adriana's eyes widened.

"I don't think something's wrong, honey. I think something's right. Piper, you're having your baby!"

Before I could protest, another contraction riddled my body, and I was sure she was right. She jumped up and ran to Ethan where he stood with his brothers, laughing about something.

He was at my side in a flash.

"How far apart are the contractions?" he asked frantically, looking at his watch.

"I don't know," I said. "They just came on really strong. Maybe it's still false labor, though."

Ethan opened his mouth to speak, but his eyes wandered down to my dress. At the same time, I felt a gush of warm water between my legs.

"And we've got ruptured membranes!" Adriana announced for everyone to hear.

"That means her water broke," Jeremy explained to the people standing around, curious about the commotion.

"Thanks for giving my family and friends a play-by-play, you guys," I said through gritted teeth.

"Okay, Piper, let's get you out of here!" Ethan said.

"It can't happen now," I wailed. "This is *our* day. We can't have a birthday and an anniversary on the same day."

"We're going to have to, honey," Ethan said, helping me outside to the car.

"I'm scared," I admitted.

"I'm here," he said. "And everyone else will be waiting outside. But we have to hurry."

The next contraction came on more powerfully than ever, and I no longer wanted to argue.

I got in the car, and he drove me to the hospital. It was strange being rolled in a wheelchair into the hospital where we both worked, but the pain was enough that I didn't pay it much mind. I was taken to the maternity ward and given a room right away.

The contractions kept coming, stronger and stronger. Dr. Conrad was notified, and she came in quickly.

"This baby wants out fast!" she exclaimed as she checked my dilation.

I lost myself in another contraction, opening my eyes only to see Ethan standing beside me. He held my hand the entire time, giving me strength and support. He was my rock.

The labor was so quick, there wasn't time to give me anything for the pain. And the pain was... intense.

But I forgot all that the moment she was born.

Before I knew it, I had a beautiful baby girl in my arms.

"Oh, my God," I breathed, while the nurses cleaned me up and rearranged everything so that we were comfortable. Ethan was close to me, and we were both bent over our new daughter, admiring what a beautiful little creature we'd created. "Hello, little girl."

"She's perfect," Ethan said. "Just like you."

"What are you going to name her?" the nurse asked.

"Savannah," I said, gazing at her angelic face.

Ethan kissed me. "Well done, sweetheart."

I squeezed his hand. "I love you, Ethan."

"I love you, too, Piper."

We exchanged a look that said more than our words ever could.

We loved each other, and now we had this precious

child that had come from that love. We had the most beautiful girl in the world, and we had each other.

There wasn't a single thing I could think of that wasn't perfect. My life had turned into a fairy tale.

And this was my incredible, wonderful, happily ever after.

COME BACK TO ME SNEAK PEEK!

Ten years ago, he crushed my heart.
Now the cocky prick is my boss.

Gavin Cole was the guy every girl wanted.
Drop-dead gorgeous with aquamarine eyes you could get lost in.
And best of all, he was mine.
Until he betrayed me with the biggest b*tch in school.
I hightailed it to Nashville and we never spoke again.

Until now.
My mom's sick. I'm back in our small town, and I need a job.
Gavin's sexier than ever. And he owns most of North Haven.
Just my luck, he's the only one hiring.
Now I have to suck up my pride and work for the man who shattered my world.
I'm not one to forgive and forget.
But when he whispers my name, my insides melt.

I want to ignore the fireworks between us, but I can't.
He's the only man to hold the key to my heart.

This could be our second chance at love...
Or maybe I'm about to get burned all over again.

Start reading *Come Back to me* NOW!

PROLOGUE

JOLIE

Ten Years Ago

The worst day of my life started out on such a high note.

I couldn't stop grinning as I waited for my boyfriend to pick me up for school. I was on top of the world, and with good reason.

A new world was right around the corner. High school graduation, freedom, and moving to the city.

Best of all, I'd be with the love of my life.

Little did I know, he was about to break my heart.

"Looking good, babe!" Gavin shouted through the open window of his truck.

He pulled his old Ford Bronco to the curb in front of my house, just as he did every morning. His blue eyes locked on mine, and my heart did a flip.

I waved goodbye to my mom, who watched from the doorway.

"Hi, Mrs. Adams!" Gavin called to her.

"You kids behave yourselves," she said, smiling, before she closed the front door.

"What are you all dressed up for?" he asked as I hopped in the passenger side.

Our friends Anna and Ryan were in the backseats. As always, the seat next to Gavin was reserved for me.

I shrugged. "It's our last week of high school. I guess I'm just excited."

I was wearing the dress he'd given me for my eighteenth birthday. It was a peach floral print that reached to my midcalf. It was just my style, even if it was fancier than what I usually wore to school.

I leaned toward Gavin and gave him a quick kiss. "Good morning!" I said brightly.

Gavin smiled. "Good morning yourself, gorgeous. Got another of those for me?"

"For you, baby? I happen to have an unlimited supply," I said.

Ryan made a gagging sound from the backseat. I ignored it. Leaning toward Gavin, I kissed him longer this time.

"Um, sorry to interrupt your tongue wrestling match," Anna said, "but could you two maybe be just a little less nauseating? I mean, my mom makes a great breakfast, but I'm not sure I feel like tasting it twice in one morning."

"Oh, you're just jealous because your boyfriend isn't as handsome as mine," I teased.

Anna turned to Ryan, elbowing him in the ribs. "Hey! Aren't you supposed to be offended by that remark?"

Ryan shrugged. "What can I say? I'm not so insecure in my masculinity that I won't admit it: Gavin's a damn good-looking guy. If I weren't straight, I'd date him."

"Gee, thanks for that, man," Gavin replied, glancing at him in the rearview mirror with an amused grimace. "If I get any unsigned cards on Valentine's Day next year, I guess I'll know where they came from, huh?"

"So, what's the news from around town today?" I asked. It was a game we often played on the way to school.

"Wow, I mean, where to start?" Gavin smirked. "The mailman was pretty sure he saw a woodchuck behind his house. They called a town meeting about that one."

"And Kurt from the hardware store bought a new weed whacker," Anna chimed in with a grin. "CNN sent a camera crew to cover that."

"Don't forget about the new coat of paint that's drying on the door of the post office," Ryan said, laughing. "Thrilling stuff. I'll definitely be watching that later, if I can handle that kind of excitement."

"God, it's going to feel so good to get out of this town and live in a real place for once!" I exclaimed happily. "After this summer, it'll be Roanoke and parties and music! No more counting off the days in a place where nothing ever happens except tourist season."

"Tourist season, ha," Ryan scoffed. "Won't be missing that either. Bunch of obnoxious out-of-towners getting drunk all summer, puking in the streets, and nearly drowning in the lake. Remember that guy who fell off the charter boat last summer? Geez."

"Those people might suck, granted," Gavin reminded him, "but without them, my dad wouldn't have made nearly as much money from all his hotels."

"Yeah, that really seemed to make him happy, too," Anna said sarcastically.

A shadow passed over Gavin's face, and we all fell into an awkward silence. His father Robert's ruthless and miserly nature had been a long-running joke in our little town of North Haven, Virginia. We had made comments like Anna's ever since we were all kids, even Gavin himself.

His dad had been the richest man in town. He'd also been the most unpopular, considered by many to be callous and greedy. He wasn't the best father to Gavin and his brothers, either.

But Gavin's parents had been killed by a drunk driver only a year before. Sometimes, it was a bit too easy for us to forget that he was still dealing with the grief.

"Hey, I'm sorry," Anna said, reaching forward and squeezing Gavin's shoulder. "That was a shitty thing for me to say."

He gave her a small smile that didn't reach his eyes. "It's okay. Really. And you're right. The fact that he's dead now doesn't mean he wasn't kind of a prick while he was alive."

I put a hand on his knee to comfort him, and he looked over at me gratefully.

"Everything's going to be okay," I told him. "Soon, we'll be off to college together, and we'll be able to put this whole place behind us and start our actual lives."

"Damn right," he said, giving me a smile. "Can't wait."

God, he was so handsome and loving and amazing. Sometimes I had a hard time believing that he was my boyfriend. How could I have been so lucky to find someone like Gavin? He'd never done anything to shake my faith in our relationship over the course of three years.

I'd found the perfect guy.

The previous month, when I had given him my virginity, he had been so gentle, so tender, so concerned with making sure I was really ready. It had been a little fumbling and awkward like most first times probably were, but it had still been amazing because it was with him.

And we had so much more of that ahead of us!

I leaned close, whispering in his ear playfully, "Soon, we won't have to sneak around after my mom goes to sleep. We can just go to each other's dorm rooms to have sex, like normal people."

He grinned from ear to ear. "I'll have to come up with some way to let my roommate know when you're there so he doesn't walk in on us."

"There's the old hang a sock on the doorknob trick," Anna suggested helpfully.

"Yeah," Ryan snickered, "or the old hang up a sign that says We're Boning In Here, Come Back In Two Minutes trick."

"You're such an asshole." Gavin laughed.

I loved his smile. I couldn't wait to spend the rest of my life doing everything I could to make sure he did it as often as possible.

First Roanoke University, I thought happily, and then the world!

He pulled into the parking lot of North Haven High, and I jumped out of the truck. "I've got to run on ahead. I did this extra credit assignment for Ms. Maxwell, and I have to get it in to her before the bell."

"Cool, I'll catch up with you later!" Gavin called after me.

"See you soon," I said as I hurried off.

I glanced back to see him bending down to inspect some minor scratch on the body of the Bronco.

Gavin's father had hated that twenty-year-old vehicle when he'd been alive. He could never understand why his son hadn't wanted something new and sleek. But Gavin loved that old truck. He'd fixed it up and made it just as nice as anything new.

"It's a classic," he'd tell anyone who would listen.

I smiled to myself. I could hardly wait for our life together to begin.

As I bounded up the front steps of the school, I started to feel weird, like everyone spoke in a whisper as soon as I'd gotten close.

I looked around.

Everyone was staring at me. Some of them appeared to be horrified, a few of them were trying to stifle laughter, but all of their eyes were on me. They all knew something I didn't.

Dread filled my chest. I didn't know what was waiting for me on the other side of that door, but something inside me was too afraid to take another step. It wanted me to turn and run away as fast as I could, to make up any excuse—that I was suddenly sick or that I had a family emergency. Anything to get away from that awful sea of eyes blinking at me.

Instead, I summoned all my courage, put my hand on the metal bar of the door, and pulled it open.

The walls and lockers were all heavily papered with copies of the same black and white photograph. Several faculty members were yanking them down by the fistful as quickly as possible, while the students just stared at them.

And at me.

"Jolie!" Ms. Maxwell hurried down the hall toward me, dropping an armload of the photos into a nearby trash can. She had a worried expression on her face. "Jolie, no, don't come in yet! Wait outside, please! Everything's all right, but just wait."

I looked at the photo on those pages. The picture was so surreal to me, so unbelievable, that it took my mind a few seconds to process it.

When I finally did—when I understood what I was looking at—I felt my entire world shatter, like a crystal ornament dropped on the floor.

Then, I did turn and run. As fast as my legs could carry me.

In some ways, I wasn't sure I ever stopped.

Start reading *Come Back to Me* NOW!

Printed in Great Britain
by Amazon

76391769R00129